I'm Still Here

A Novel

K.G. Miceli

Table Of Contents

I felt its eyes on me. Taunting.

Inside, I long for a world where there is peace.

I long for a world where these demons don't exist.

I long for the impossible.

1

I flipped through the channels on the TV in my family's living room, settling on an episode of *Oprah.* They were speaking something about personal styling and makeovers, something that I was *barely* ever interested in. Unfortunately, we only had cable and there wasn't much to choose from.

I was trying to make sense of the episode, when I heard my mother and sister arguing upstairs.

They were always arguing.

It was always over nonsense, like who left the butter out, or why did you use my hairbrush when you have your own?

Talks of blue eye-shadow mixed with sparkles were washed out by the sounds of yelling and things being tossed.

Great, I thought. *Not again.*

I was so fed up with my sister, always trying to pick fights with my mom, always making such a big deal out of nothing. And for what? To make my mother cry and hide away all day? To make her want to run away?

"No!" I could hear my sister yell, followed by the sound of what must have been a purse or a jacket hitting a wall. "I'm not going and that's that!"

I rolled my eyes, grabbing for the remote to turn the television volume up.

Just as I was about to click the little plus button, I could hear footsteps approaching, thudding into the hardwood.

Oh my God, just leave me out of it.

I knew that one of them would be on their way to me, to whine and complain about the other, to tell me why they were angry.

It had been such a long day at school that all I wanted to do was sit there and relax in silence.

I had exams in every subject, projects that I had just finished and handed in. It may have been the last day of school, but that didn't mean that I didn't deserve to take just a small breather.

I just wanted them to leave me out of their argument, just this once at least.

I looked over to see my mother entering the room, her steps now more subtle. I was expecting to see a look of sadness, or anger, but instead I could only make out urgency.

My eyes locked onto hers as I wondered what she had come to say. Did I do something wrong? Did something happen?

Just as I was about to ask, she spoke.

"Claire," she hesitated. "Claire, we're gonna be moving. I know you have a lot of friends here, but your dad has to move for work. It's a really nice place. I have pictures if you want to see?"

At first, I didn't know what to say.

My father was a cruise line worker, so I had always known that there was the possibility of having to relocate. He was always gone, working long hours and days out on the coast near Portland in Maine state.

He was only ever seldom able to find time to come home, maybe only a few times a month. It had felt almost as if our family was broken, most of my mom's nights were spent lying awake hoping that he would walk in through the front door. My sister was always trying to act like the world owed her something, like she had forgotten that she was only thirteen.

As his daughter, of course I missed him too, but I tried to stay away from home most days to keep my mind occupied. I spent most of my free time out at the mall with Carissa, and the other girls from school. We would go for walks down near the boat docks, sometimes we drank I'll admit, other days we would work on homework. Something about hearing the waves crashing against the rock walls had always helped me concentrate.

I thought about how I would tell my friends that I had to leave so suddenly. I knew that they wouldn't be very impressed and truth be told, I really wasn't either.

We had only lived in Portland for around two years and I was just starting to get more comfortable, just beginning to admit that this was home.

I grew irritated with the thought of having to move all over again, having to start my last year of high school in a whole new district. I would have to meet new people, make new friends and be the "new kid" again, and I loathed that feeling.

"No, Mom, I don't want to see pictures. It's not like it matters," I snapped more than I had intended. "Just tell me when I have to have my things packed by."

I studied her to find that she looked frustrated, too.

Her eyes moved slowly to the floor, leaving my gaze as she let out a sigh.

"Tomorrow."

Tomorrow? I thought. *How could they have had less than a twenty four hour notice?*

Without even meaning to, I rolled my eyes and scoffed.

I felt the anger that I had fought so hard to push away begin to rise up within me. It didn't make any sense. *Tomorrow?*

It was much too soon. How would I tell Carissa that I would probably never be able to see her again?

Then I understood why my sister had been so displeased, why she was yelling and carrying on.

"Seriously?" I asked, watching her as her eyes met mine again and she motioned to respond. "Never mind. I'll go pack."

I set the remote down on the end table beside me, controlling myself not to throw it across the room, and stood up.

I walked past my mother, who was still standing in the same position as before. I avoided eye contact as I stomped into the hallway and up the stairs.

"I don't want to leave either, Claire. But this place is really nice, you'll see."

I could hear her speaking from the bottom of the stairs.

I didn't want to talk about it, I just wanted her to drop the subject and let me go pack in peace so I could cool off.

I opened the door to my bedroom, making my way to the foot of my bed and sat down.

Tomorrow? What the hell!

I took a look around, glancing at everything that I would have to pack. All of my make-up sat on the desk, jewellery and clothes sat upon my dresser, clothing piled lazily into a hamper that sat next to the door.

There wasn't a whole lot, but I knew that it would take me at least a few hours.

Might as well do it now.

I pulled a small plastic tote bin out from underneath my bed and held it in my hands, glancing around the room for something that would fit inside. Jewellery.

I stood up from my bed and decided that I had to get it done.

* * *

"Dinner!" I heard my mom call from downstairs, just as I had finished packing the last box.

I hadn't even thought about food, but the word made me realize that I was starving.

Setting the box that I was holding into the pile of others, I made my way for the door and then headed downstairs.

On the main floor, it smelled of something sweet, with garlic maybe? My mouth began to water.

As I got to the kitchen table, I saw my mother standing, hunched over the stove, pulling something from the oven.

Mmm, stuffed peppers! My favourite.

I pulled out a chair and took a seat next to my sister.

She was sitting, one hand on the table and the other grasping her cell phone, probably checking on her social media accounts.

There was seldom ever a time that she did not have that thing in her hand, most people would have thought that it was attached to her.

"Stuffed peppers, girls," my mother announced, squeezing her way in between us and spooning out a big, over-filling pepper onto the plates that sat in front of us. "Eat up! Big day tomorrow!"

I tried to think of a way to respond that wouldn't arise another argument, but there was nothing I could say. I only sat there, staring at the food that sat in front of me.

As I picked up my fork, I could hear my sister mumble something under her breath, something about moving, but I couldn't make out the words.

"What was that Elizabeth?" My mother ushered her to speak, and I knew that it was better if she didn't.

I wanted to, at least, have one more dinner together in this house, our home, before we would have no choice but to experience an entirely new life.

Just don't say anything. I found myself thinking, hoping somehow Liz would hear my thoughts. *Please.*

I could see my sister's arm tense up through the corner of my eye. She kept her eyes on her phone, trying to ignore my mom and I, both.

I stuck my fork into the mound of ground beef, bread crumbs and sauce that sat on my plate, pulling out a chunk, and then brought it to my mouth.

The taste was just as I expected, just like my mom had always made them.

I could feel my taste buds screaming with glee as I finished the delicious piece of food.

I looked up to my mother, who was still staring at Elizabeth, her eyes filled with a fury that I couldn't quite place.

"The food is really good, mom. Thank you," I said, trying to defuse the situation.

She turned herself to face me, her expression switching to some sort of pride.

"Thank you, Claire," she responded gently.

There was a slight awkward silence as I ate my food, Elizabeth still ignoring hers, and scrolling through her phone.

Ignoring my sister, I decided that I was a little bit curious about where we were moving. I wondered what city we would be moving to, how big the house was, how nice the house might be.

"Do you have those pictures, mom?"

I could see her face light up as she set her apron down and pulled a chair out, taking a seat beside me. She pulled her phone out from her pocket.

"It's beautiful... and the best part is, it's not in a city! Our first country home, Claire!"

She clicked a few things on her phone, her fingers swiping across the screen.

Her purple nail polish almost seemed to disappear with how quickly she was swiping.

She finally stopped and settled on an image, handing the phone out towards me.

I looked at her, and then to the phone, setting my fork down onto my plate. Reaching over, I pulled the phone from her hand, my eyes locking onto the photo on the screen.

It was a photo of what looked like a kitchen, a clean, old-fashioned room. The floor was made up of hardwood, all of the cupboards, even the table, were a beautiful maple brown. It looked something like that of an old palace. A large chandelier hung from the ceiling, candles lit and sitting inside of it, a beautiful candelabra sat in the middle of the table.

The house suddenly didn't seem so terrible, but something about it made me feel slightly off, uneasy even. I was sure that it was most likely just the darkness in the photo and the lack of lighting.

"Do you have more pictures?" I asked, becoming more intrigued.

She brought her finger back to the phone, still in my hand, and swiped over just once.

The living room.

There were two panoply figures in the back corners of the room, each holding a shield and a large sword up to their chests. The mantles were littered with beeswax candles and old gas lanterns, unlit. There was something about the suits, something about the room that sent a chill down my spine. I didn't know why, as it all looked so beautiful. Maybe it was just because it was a style that I had never been accustomed to.

She scrolled over to the next photo that looked like it must have been a basement, it was dark and empty. I couldn't make out a single thing in the picture.

"What's this?" I asked, glancing over to my mother.

She leaned her head in, trying to get a better view of the photo.

"I don't know, I didn't notice that one in there before," she stared at the image, as if expecting it to suddenly change, or something.

"That's weird," I looked back down to the photo, studying the darkness, trying to spot something.

There was a closed door at the very back of the picture, the only light present was what had crept in through the crack between the door and the floor. It looked like unfinished wood, maybe? I wasn't sure.

Trying to find a trace of something, I noticed two small red lights glowing, side by side in the blackness.

They didn't light up any area around them, and I couldn't place exactly what I was looking at. Was it some sort of movie player? Lights from a TV that was powered off? I didn't know, but the more that I watched them, the more that they began to look like glowing eyes.

2

After dinner, I decided that I would call Carissa and let her know that I was going to be leaving.

It didn't really matter what reaction she would have, since I didn't have a choice, and I could only hope that she would realize that and not take it out on me.

I sprawled myself out on my bed and pulled out my phone, stretching out my arms and letting out a yawn. I was exhausted, and even more so, dreading the phone call that I was about to make.

I opened my phone and clicked the icon of her photo and then hit the little green phone icon.

Riiing. Riiing.

I was greeted with a high pitched "Claiiiiire!"

My ears rang as I pulled the phone just slightly away from my face.

She was always so excited and giddy, some days it was too much for me, other days I played along.

She was one of those "party girls" that always wanted to be doing something, she never liked to relax or just spend a day in, and sometimes I wished that she would. Her mother was an alcoholic and her father left when she was just a baby, so in a way, I did feel sympathetic towards her.

"What's up, girl?" She shrieked. "Wanna come hang?"

She sounded hopeful, but I was too tired to want to do anything.

"No, sorry, I can't tonight."

"Well, what's up then? Everything okay?"

I sighed, trying to think of the words to say.

I'm leaving tomorrow, and I'm probably not going to be back. No, way too harsh. *I'm sorry, Carissa, but I'll see you again soon.*

I let out a groan that she could probably hear, and returned to the phone.

"Listen, I don't know how to tell you this... but," I started, and then she cut me off.

"You bought those shoes that I wanted? Girl, no, I was going to buy those for the party next week."

Oh crap. The party.

I had promised her about a week back that I would attend the end of school party with her that was being thrown by the seniors. We had made plans that my mom was supposed to drive me and pick her up along the way. We even picked out our outfits, trying to collaborate our styles.

This made matters worse, since now I had to tell her that she would have to find another way there, and another party date as well.

"No. No, actually about that I..."

"Okay, good! 'Cause I really need those ones to go with my dress, and hey! You'll never guess who's coming!"

She always tended to ramble, rarely letting me get even a word in at times.

I didn't have a choice but to shoot her down before she built up even more excitement within herself. I felt horrible, but what else was I to do?

"Carissa, shut up and listen to me."

I cut her off, my words tearing through the room, creating a silence that I didn't expect.

Carissa stopped talking, leaving only the sound of her breathing through the phone.

"I'm moving, Car. I don't have a choice, I have to go," I could hear my own voice breaking up into pieces.

I knew that we were leaving, but it was different hearing those words escape my mouth. It brought a reality to the situation that I hadn't felt before.

I waited for a response, and for what seemed like minutes, there wasn't any. I couldn't hear a single sound on the other side of the phone call. *Had she hung up?*

As I pulled the phone away from my face to see if we were still connected I heard a loud, ear piercing screech coming from my phone.

Carissa. She was wailing in a way I had never heard and I wondered if she had hurt herself, or if this was the result of my news.

I waited for the sound to stop, and then placed the phone back up to my ear.

"You alright, Car?" I asked.

No response.

"Car, what the hell."

I was just about to hang up and attempt to call her back when her voice returned to the phone.

"When? Where are you going? Why? What?"

I could hear her sniffling, her words choked and hoarse.

"Tomorrow," I answered sternly. "We're moving to Massachusetts, to the country there."

She continued to sob as I stared blankly at my bedroom ceiling, wondering how living in the country would be.

I had always been a city girl, I was born and raised in the city. Any time we had ever moved, it was never close to the country at all. How would I get used to the complete silence that would accompany the new house, the open back fields, the wild animals that might lurk outside?

I wasn't exactly sure, but I knew that it was going to take some getting used to.

I was beginning to think she was never going to stop crying, and that I was eventually going to have to hang up on her, when she suddenly spoke.

"So, what about the party then? Guess I'll find my own ride... thank you for calling me. Can you try to come back and see me?"

"Of course I'll try," I stated.

And I meant it, I really did want to come back.

"I'm going to head off to bed tho Car, call me tomorrow night after I get there?"

"Sure."

I heard the chime of the phone call disconnect and pulled the phone away from my ear, setting it down on the desk beside my bed.

I clicked off the lamp on the desk, submerging the room into darkness. Rolling over, I pulled the blankets over one shoulder and turned to face the wall.

I began thinking of the new house, running the photos I had seen through my mind. I was thinking of the beautiful kitchen with the nice hardwood floors, the medieval style living room filled with candles and antique lamps. The dark room, that strange, dark room. A basement? An attic? A bedroom, maybe? The red eye-shaped spots in the corner of the room, watching, waiting, threatening even. How had that photo gone unnoticed? Surely, it was sent by a Realtor? A TV. Just a DVD player. Maybe it was something much, much more evil.

3

I was awoken by the sound of a large engine humming just outside my window. It rattled, the vibrations echoing through my room, off the walls and into my ears.

Forcing myself to open my eyes, I found that the light was blinding. A bright white light engulfed my retinas as I pushed myself to open them.

It was extremely sunny out, which was a relief from the constant cloudiness that had overtaken the sky for the past weeks. I sat up and threw the covers off of my legs, half of them falling onto the floor.

Tiredly, I set one foot on the ground, noticing that the hardwood had been unusually warm. My eyes were still adjusting to the light, as I fixated them on the solo window that sat just above my dresser.

As the humming continued, I realized what it most likely was, *the moving truck.*

I rubbed my eyes, and forced them to adjust, a long yawn escaping my mouth.

Standing up, I made my way to the dresser, and pulled out the outfit that I had left unpacked for the day.

I peered out through the window to see a large box truck idling in the driveway.

I could see my mom rushing items out of the house and into the back of the truck. Kitchen chairs and boxes, lots of boxes.

Might as well get the show on the road, I told myself.

Pulling away from the window, I got myself dressed, ignoring the sounds of my sister struggling to bring things down the stairs from her bedroom.

What better weather for jeans and a hoodie? I thought. I threw on my favourite, most comfortable hoodie that I owned and headed for the door, grabbing two boxes along the way.

I headed down the stairs, struggling to keep my balance as I descended, the box threatening to slip from within my grasp. I had misjudged the weight and probably should have only grabbed one.

At the bottom of the stairs, I noticed that the house was practically already empty. All of the furniture that had once made up our home was replaced with empty corners and dust bunnies.

I regained control of the box and headed for the front door. Through the living room, I could hear a slight banging and the shuffling of cardboard. Turning the corner, I could see my mom loading both of her arms up to full capacity.

How could such a small woman carry so many boxes, when I had struggled just to carry two?

I was heading for the door when she lifted her head.

"Claire! You're up!" She stated, as if it weren't obvious.

I stopped and looked at her, still slightly groggy. My eyes darted from wall to wall, realizing how much she had already done.

"Did I sleep in? What time is it?" I asked sincerely. "You could have woken me up to help."

She sighed.

"I wanted to let you sleep, it's going to be a long day."

Looking up to where the clock had usually sat upon the wall, I realized that she must have already packed it away.

"It's nearly noon," she informed me. "It's fine though, really."

I didn't know what else to say, my mom was stubborn some days, and refused to ask for help even when she needed it most.

"Okay... thanks mom."

As I was about to head for the door again, my sister walked in, pushing past me and nudging me with her shoulder. The box that I was holding fell to the floor as I tried to catch it.

Was that the box that I had put my glass knickknacks in?

I bent over and lifted a corner of the box. *No, just clothes.*

"Thanks, *asshole,*" I snarled, picking up the box.

Turning to me only slightly and giving me a glare, she turned back around and continued to the stairs.

"Your welcome."

Your welcome? I swear I could have hit her.

"Girls, girls. We have enough time to argue in the car on the way there. Let's just get this done," my mother chimed in.

Ignoring the anger building up inside me, I headed out the door.

Outside was not too warm, yet not too cold. A beautiful autumn day.

Making my way to the back of the truck, I tossed the boxes inside and slid them over to make sure that there was still room for more.

The truck was already about three quarters full, and I couldn't imagine that there would be much more to add.

* * *

"Alright, that's the last box!" My mom announced.

Dusting off her hands onto her jeans, she closed the back doors to the truck, a heavy thud following.

She smacked the side of the box three times, and I watched as the truck slowly started to accelerate out of the drive and down the road, speeding away into the city traffic.

"Are we going now?" I asked, half excitedly, and half with dread.

Pulling the keys out from her front pocket, she gave me a look of please. She smiled as she shook the car keys in front of my face, and then began walking to the car.

I sighed and turned around.

"So long," I whispered, as if the house could somehow hear me or respond. "Goodbye, home."

I found that I was staring at the red brick, stuck in a sort of trance.

Snap shots of good times flipped through my memory.

I remembered when my sister and I had arrived there for the very first time. Though we were filled with uncertainty of what the place would hold, we had tried to make the most of it. We had explored the neighbourhood, finding the trails that laid hidden away. I remembered the old oak tree at the end of one of the paths that became our comfort spot. Any time one of us were upset, that was surely where you could have found us.

I remembered my dad coming home from one of his cruises and taking us all out for ice cream. Liz's had fallen off the cone and onto her shirt, staining the white polyester. She didn't complain, she didn't freak out, she was much different back then. Instead, a grin spread across her face as she let out a wail of laughter.

"Are you talking to the house?" A voice emerged from behind me, startling me, as I snapped back to reality.

"You're freaking weird."

It was Elizabeth.

I thought about turning around and starting an argument. *You're weird.* I thought, but I decided to bite my tongue. There was no point in getting her all worked up, since I had to spend my next hours stuck in the car with her.

I wouldn't be able to just turn away and go up to my bedroom. I wouldn't be able to hide away with my music cranked, drowning away all of my thoughts.

I turned around to face her, rolling my eyes at her, intentionally.

She didn't say anything, she only looked back to her phone and turned back for the car.

I could see my mother in the front seat, her blonde hair pulled up into a ponytail, her head bobbing up and down as her mouth moved.

Great. We get to listen to eighties music.

I headed for the vehicle, trying my hardest not to look back.

This is it. Just don't look back.

If only I had found a way to stay. If only I could have convinced my mom not to leave. If only I could have known that this was the very beginning of something dreadful.

4

I pulled out my headphones, attempting to untangle the cord. *Girls just wanna have fun* played throughout the car, and I longed for it to stop.

Throwing my headphones on over my head, I flipped through the music playlist on my phone.

I settled for some *Avenged Sevenfold* and laid my head back, resting it against the back of the seat.

The car started off, the whirring of tires against the road picked up. I peered out through the window beside me, and took one last look at the house.

And that was it, I never did see my home again after that.

* * *

The drive seemed endless.

In the city, at least there were things to see. Busy shops, merchandise sitting just outside their doors, there were people walking their dogs, beautiful gardens and storefronts.

Here, there was nothing. Empty fields replaced buildings and apartments, unkempt long weeds replaced the grass that would have been cut daily. There were few trees as most of the fields stood empty and endless, others held vegetation.

The highway seemed to go on forever, like an endless black strip of tar that wrapped around the earth.

I glanced over to my sister who had been sitting quietly, eyes still glued to her phone.

I missed who she was before, who she was before she had started high school.

It was almost as if she had transformed into a completely different person, but from time to time, I could still see the real Liz in there. My little sister.

I hated how she wouldn't talk to me anymore, how she would take every emotion that she felt inside, and bottle it away.

I felt if she would just open up, and talk to me, that I might have been able to help with whatever she was going through, but that involved her not being so closed off.

She must have felt my stare on her as she turned and gave me a scowl.

"Liz?" I asked, pulling my headphones down and resting them on the back of my neck.

Her eyes turned to me, only slightly, as she pretended that she didn't hear.

I watched her for a few seconds, studying her to see if she would answer. Still, she acted as though I didn't exist.

"Liz."

This time her eyes left her phone, turning to lock onto mine. In her face I could sense disgust, loathing even.

What was her problem with me?

"Why are you so rude all the time? Like... are you okay?" I asked sincerely.

She didn't respond right away. As she hesitated and then looked down to her phone again, I didn't think she was going to answer me.

To my surprise, she clicked the button on her phone, causing the back light to go out, and then looked back to me.

"You never cared before, so why do you now?" She answered. There was a condescending look in her eyes.

I didn't know how to answer that. I had always cared about her.

It was hard to make her understand, since I may have led her to believe that I didn't care. She came home one day, completely out of the blue with a chip on her shoulder.

I could still remember that day like it had just happened. One moment, we were so close, going for walks together, sharing our happenings of the day. We would talk about everything and share our deepest darkest secrets. The next moment, she had walked in the door after school a whole new person.

I was home sick with the flu, grabbing a cold glass of water. She had walked in and thrown her bag down on the kitchen table with such a force that the contents spilled out across it and onto the floor.

"What's wrong?" I had asked her, seriously worried.

"Fuck you."

That was the response I had received.

I could remember watching her push past my mother and stomp through the room, up the stairs and then disappearing to her bedroom.

Ever since that day, it was like some kind of demon had taken over her, creating her to lash out, and hurt everyone in her path.

I wondered if I really wanted to find out what had happened that day. Part of me just wanted to let it be.

"I always did care, but you turned into a complete asshole. What do you expect me to do? Kiss your feet?"

I couldn't control it anymore, it was like there was a volcano inside me just waiting to erupt.

She shook her head and turned back to her phone.

"You wouldn't understand."

She spoke without so much as looking up, her fingers scrolling up and down on her screen.

I tried to remember if there was something I had done to set her off. Had I done something at school? Maybe someone had told her some story that wasn't true?

I didn't know, but I desperately wanted to figure it out.

"Then let me understand," I mumbled, turning to face my window. "I can't understand what I don't know."

"You should help us out, Elizabeth," I heard my mom chime in from the driver's seat.

Great.

I didn't want her to get involved, it seemed as though almost all of Liz's rage was directed toward her. I didn't want to have to deal with one of their screaming matches while trapped within the confinement of the car.

Thankfully, neither of them spoke again.

I rested myself against the back of the seat and closed my eyes.

There was no point in trying to get any more out of my sister, so I decided that maybe a nap would be best. It was still such a long way to our new place.

* * *

I was awoken to the startling sound of a horn blaring, tires screeching across the asphalt.

I nearly jumped out of my skin as I opened my eyes and to my horror, I could see the front end of a tractor trailer headed directly for us.

The truck appeared to be in the wrong lane, our lane.

I could hear metal on metal, as the truck attempted to break, swerving only slightly to the left.

My mother pressed onto the car horn, over and over, holding it down in long strides, as if it were to change any outcome we would face.

As she turned the steering wheel sharply to the right, I could see Liz's petrified face from the corner of my eyes, her lips tensed in fear, eyes sealed shut.

She looked exactly as I had felt.

The vehicle seemed to move so slowly, making it's way to the dirt shoulder of the road, spraying rocks and dust up as we flew into it.

My face made contact with the back of the passenger seat, sending a jolt of pain up into my head. I could feel my nose crack with the pressure, as a warm feeling followed.

The car continued to roll, shaking me around like a rag doll. At some point my head must have hit the headliner as I struggled to stay in my seat.

I tried to see out of the window, but everything was moving so fast that I couldn't make out a single thing.

There was a loud thud as the vehicle came to a halt, my head hitting the seat one final time, pain dispersing throughout my entire body.

And then everything went black.

5

Beep. Beep. Beep.

Where am I? What happened?

Beep. Beep. Beep.

My eyes felt heavy as I tried to force them open, feeling around for anything, or anyone.

Beep. Beep. Beep.

I could feel something on the tip of my finger, pressure that suddenly made me so uncomfortable.

I reached for my hand and ripped off the piece of plastic that had been gripping me so tightly, tossing it to the floor.

As it hit the floor, the sound reminded me of what had happened last.

A car accident?

Finally, I was able to force my eyes open, the blinding white lights made it hard to adjust.

As I struggled to regain my sight, I could hear voices, sounds and machines not very far away. They echoed as they carried over to where I laid.

The hospital, I realized.

The machine that was making such an ungodly sound finally subsided.

I could see above me, a beige ceiling that looked as though it had previously been white. There were splotches of what looked to be coffee stains just above my head, although I knew that it was probably caused from something much, much more distasteful.

As I turned my head to face the monitors, pain shot up my neck. My face was sore, as if there were a hundred scrapes, and my arm felt as though it were on fire.

"Ow!" I hollered, louder than I had meant to.

I could see the monitors. A few of them were completely shut off, others flashed red.

I glanced over to see a beautiful set of stargazer lilies, yellows, purples and beautiful pinks mixed with whites.

Those had been my favourite flowers, ever since my dad had picked some up on one of his cruises and brought them home to me.

It was one of the small memories that I had always cherished.

Next to the vase sat a white card, folded in half, along with a coffee cup.

Curious about the note, and longing for caffeine, I decided to sit myself up.

The sheets were thin and coarse, not the most comfortable thing that I had ever slept under. I found it hard to move, as I threw an arm to my side, attempting to thrust myself upwards. It was when I had tried to move my other arm, that I had noticed the heavy weight, forcing it to fall back down to the bed, followed by a stinging pain.

Removing my eyes from the table, I looked down to see a large white cast, spreading it's way from my wrist up to my elbow.

I rubbed my good hand along it, allowing the rough texture to force me back into reality.

Is it broken? I wondered. *What else had happened?*

I reached my hand up to my face, and discovered that there were bandages taped across my nose. As I touched it, I realized that it didn't hurt nearly as much as my arm.

There was a cut that I could feel just above my upper lip, the synthetic wire of stitches grazing my fingertips. There were a few other minor scrapes and sore spots that I was sure were probably bruises.

Turning my gaze back to the table, I lifted my cast up, supporting it with my other hand and was able to move.

I managed to shift my way upwards, thrusting with all of my weight.

With my eyes still stuck on the table, I threw my legs off the side of the bed.

It was hard to stand, at first I almost fell, stumbling forwards and then balancing myself on one of the monitors.

As I tried to make my way forward, I felt an unforgiving tug at my wrist. I glanced down to see an IV emerging from beneath my skin, the tape half torn off. Small drops of blood mixed with saline solution rolled down my arm and dripped onto the tile.

"Shit!" I said aloud, attempting to throw my hand across to cover the wound, but it was no use.

The cast was far too heavy and I was too weak. It hurt as I let my arm back down, stumbling backwards and catching myself on the bed.

I could see the stand that held the bag of solution, the line running down to the floor and then up into my body.

Without thinking, I grabbed a hold of the tube that was lodged into me and pulled.

The feeling was disturbing. The sense of complete pressure, and then none at all, made me instantly nauseous. Blood dripped out as I set the tube down on the bed beside me. Both of my arms throbbed with pain.

I stood there, leaning against the edge of the bed for a few seconds, trying to regain control and then attempted once more to make it to the table.

I picked myself up, much more stability this time and walked over to the table.

My legs felt as though I was lugging heavy bags of sand beneath me, forcing them to move in ways that they refused to go.

I was frustrated, after what felt like hours of attempts, but I had finally made it to the table.

I set my hand down on the card. A wave of relief swept over me when I caught a glimpse of my wrist. The blood that had been pouring out had subsided.

I picked up the small piece of paper. Right away, I could see handwriting on the front of the card, writing that I recognized.

Claire, it read.

It was my Mom's writing. At least I felt better knowing that she made it out of the accident in good shape, since she was still able to write so neatly.

I opened up the card.

Claire.
I'm so sorry, honey.
This is all my fault.
Please forgive me.
Call a nurse when you wake up,

me and Elizabeth will be right there to see you.
I'll be in every few hours with a fresh coffee.
Hope you're up soon.
I love you, sweet heart.
Love, Mom.

Well, at least I knew that my mother and sister were safe, but then arose my next question.

How long was I out?

I wasn't sure if I even wanted to know. Had I passed out, or was it some sort of coma?

I could only hope that I hadn't been asleep for too long.

I was lost in thought when I heard the door handle turn. The door swung open and a tiny, older lady walked in.

She wore a set of purple scrubs, her black hair pulled up into a bun, her eyes studied the clipboard she had been holding in her hands.

I stood there, wondering what to say when she looked up and inhaled deeply, her hand settling over her chest.

Her eyes were wide, her expression frightened as she locked eyes onto mine from the doorway.

I could see her quivering as I set down the note and stared at her.

"You're... You're up!" She stated, as if it weren't already obvious. "When did you wake up? You should have hit the button!"

Truth be told, I didn't even notice a button.

"I..." I started, my voice dry. "Only a few minutes."

My eyes left hers, as I looked to the coffee cup beside me, I was so unbelievably thirsty.

I reached over and picked it up, rolling the cup back and forth within my grip, longing to take a sip.

I could hear the scratching of the pen against the clipboard, and I wondered what she was writing.

I pulled back the tab on my cup and popped it open, leaning it towards my mouth for a sip as, my eyes darted back to hers.

"How are you feeling?" She asked, sternly, without much of a trace of concern.

I allowed myself a sip. Black coffee poured into me as I felt myself come a little bit more to life.

It was cold, not as I had expected, and I wondered how long it had been since my mom had been in to see me.

"I'm alright... my arm is sore, but I can't really feel much else. Where is my mother?"

She stopped writing and studied me for a moment.

"She was in before noon this morning. I'm sure she'll be back within the hour, but I'll give her a call and let her know you're up."

I nodded, taking my coffee and stumbling back towards the bed.

"You should relax until she gets back," she suggested, making her way over to me. She set her pen behind her ear and stuck her clipboard under her armpit, grabbing my arm and lifting it around her shoulders. "You shouldn't be up walking around so soon."

I allowed her to assist me, although the urge to push her away and take off out through the door made me hesitate. I didn't want to be stuck there.

"Where are we?" I asked. "How long have I been here?"

She let my arm down, allowing me to sit gently onto the side of the mattress.

"You're in Worcester. At Saint Vincent hospital." Her eyes moved gently away from mine, settling onto the sheets that were sprawled across the bed, half laying on the floor. "You've been in a coma for three days."

Three days, Massachusetts?

I wondered if my mother had already gone to the new house, if she had seen it yet. I wondered if they had expected me to survive, or if I was only at this point, a lost cause.

Nevertheless, I felt slightly relieved that they hadn't forgotten about me, that my mother had still come in to make sure I had a somewhat fresh coffee, just in case I had woken up. I was glad that they had stuck around for me.

Puzzled, I could only sit there, trying to figure out how three days had passed without me having any recollection of any of it.

A coma?

There was nothing to start off this new chapter of my life like a coma. And maybe it would have been better if I hadn't woken up at all.

6

The nurse left the room, mumbling something about making a phone call. I sprawled myself out across the bed, laying there like a piece of laundry waiting to be folded.

I stared up at the ceiling. My mind was a mess as I tried to piece things together, to figure out what the last thing that I remembered was.

The rolling of the car, the darkness that had taken over my view from outside the window. The sheering pain bolting through my head and down, spreading throughout my entire body. Mud. I could remember seeing mud before everything had gone black. Had we crashed into a field? A ditch?

I convinced myself that it didn't really matter anymore, but one thing that stood out in my mind was that tractor trailer. I couldn't remember hearing the sound of the truck contacting with our vehicle, so, surely my mom had avoided the head on collision...

That was good, right?

I wondered if the car was still intact, or if it had already been written off by the insurance. I wondered if my sister had sustained any injuries from the impact, my mother?

I figured that my side of the car must have gotten the majority of the damage, and that maybe they were completely fine, and had gotten out without so much as a scratch. All I could do was hope.

I was startled by the sound of footsteps just outside my door, voices carried through. I didn't recognize the voice of the elderly woman that had been speaking, but I could make out that one of them belonged to my mother.

Sitting up, I could see the handle turn. The door began to inch open only slightly and I watched as it slowly stopped.

The voices continued.

I felt my jaw drop open slightly as I tried to regain control of it. I longed for my mom, even just for a familiar face, a familiar voice. At that point, I would have even loved to see Liz. I could have put up with her attitude for a while, just to get some normalcy back.

"The nurse said she looked good, she's just a little bit weak. The wounds on her face are healing well, but the arm's gonna be a couple of weeks."

"Okay, thank you, doctor."

I could hear my mom conversing with the staff outside my door. A silhouette of a woman stood just outside.

The door creaked open and that was when I saw her.

Elizabeth, my mother trailing behind her as they entered the room.

I could see a look of concern on Liz's face, not the everyday look that I had expected to see instead. My mother looked relieved, as she wiped a few tears away from her cheeks.

Both of their eyes met mine as they began to speak at the same time.

"Claire! How are..."

"Oh my God, You're oka..."

And then they both went silent. Liz was the first to stand at my side, as she studied me in astonishment. My mom came to stand on the other side of me, grabbing at my arm that bore the cast.

"Ouch," I mumbled, pulling my arm away slightly, as to not hurt it any further.

She stopped and let me go, pulling her hands back to herself.

"I'm sorry, Claire! I'm just so worried, I wanted to check it."

I sighed.

"It's in a cast, you can't really see."

We stayed motionless for a few seconds, my mom continuing to wipe tears of relief from her face.

Elizabeth only stood there, staring at me as if she were seeing a ghost.

"You passed out when you hit your head... they said there was a small chance that you wouldn't wake up," Liz spoke, and it was the first time in years that I had heard anything within her voice other than hatred. "I was so worried."

I didn't know what to say to her, somehow, I was surprised that she had cared, that she had worried.

I lifted my hand to my face, rubbing my fingers along the stitches that sat within my skin.

"Can I go home?" I asked.

I had never liked hospitals. The very smell made me want to vomit, the sounds of monitors and cart wheels against tile gave me a pounding headache. Chatter from the hallways, that always seemed to carry to every corner of each room, felt unbearable. I just wanted to get out of there.

"Yes, honey." My mother answered, I turned back to face her. "We can, they just want about another half hour to make sure that you are really okay. You had a little bit of internal bleeding. It's better now, but they just need to make sure you don't fall back asleep before we go."

Fall back asleep? Pass out, you mean. Go back into a coma, you mean.

I let out a long breath of air, the hair from my head that had fallen over my face moved with it.

"Fine..." I answered, removing my gaze from my mother and settling it back onto the door.

"It won't be long, and we'll stay here with you. We've been staying in a hotel, and I already called to let them know we don't need it anymore. I went to the house this morning, and oh, Claire, it's beautiful. It's even more lovely than in the photos," her voice trailed off.

"You guys didn't have to do that. What if I wouldn't have woken up at all?"

I paused, and thought about how easily that could have happened.

Only hours ago, I was moments away from death's door. So easily, I could have been pulled away from this world, and thrown into another. How easily I could have been six feet deep, instead of sitting there, alive. And suddenly, the hospital didn't even seem so bad anymore.

"I wanted to wait for you to see it before we went. It didn't seem right going without you. But the good news is, it's only about an hour's drive outside the city. I let your dad know what happened, he's stuck on a cruise right now, but

I'm going to call and let him know that you're alright. I can't wait to get you home."

Uggh. A drive.

That was the last thing that I wanted to do, and I wished that there was some way we could have just walked.

7

The next hour had gone by quite quickly. Most of it was spent with my mother, resting her head against my shoulder, my sister playing on her cell phone.

I stared at the door, as the nurse that had been in to see me last time barged in with the discharge papers.

Finally.

My mother signed a few lines as the nurse continued to hand an endless amount sheets.

"And sign here please. If she starts feeling really dizzy, or loses consciousness at all make sure you bring her right back in."

She finished signing everything, handing it back to the nurse who then placed the documents onto her clipboard.

"And you're good to go. We'll mail the bill."

I didn't even want to think of how much money I was going to cost my family. I would have offered to help pay, but with no job or money saved, there was little to nothing that I would have been able to do.

I tried to sit up, as Elizabeth shoved her phone into her side pocket, and helped me stabilize myself.

"Thanks, Liz," I said, struggling to my feet.

We headed for the door as my mother finished up with the nurse.

As we exited the room, and started down the long busy hallway, my mother's footsteps trailed behind us.

The were doctors rushing around, paperwork in hand. There were nurses conversing into groups, chatter echoed throughout the brightly lit up space.

As we walked past a custodian, mop in hand, I gathered the strength to let my arm free of Liz. I walked beside her the rest of the way to the elevators, as my mother stepped up beside me.

She hit the button to go down, it glowed a dull orange.

"You ready?" She asked, as if I had a choice if I wasn't.

"Sure," I replied solemnly, glancing to the elevator door.

There was a short pause, followed by the chime of an electronic bell, as the elevator thudded into place.

The sound made me think of all those horror movies, ones where the elevator would break and the characters would plunge to their deaths. I thought of the doors closing on one of us, just when we would try to enter. I thought of the doors never opening back up, and us left there to die, slowly. But I quickly shook my head, as if that were to make the thoughts fly away.

The stainless steel doors slowly slid open. There was an elderly lady, sitting in a wheelchair, a middle aged woman standing behind her.

I waited patiently, as they exited the elevator, the younger lady pushing the wheelchair out and walking past us. She gave a slight smile as they past, as if to say *have a great day!*

I smiled back, and stepped into the elevator, my shoes sounding weighted as I stepped onto the metal platform.

Once inside, I noticed a man. Something about him was strange. *Very strange.*

He stood motionless, directly in the corner closest to the buttons near the door.

He wore a long black hoodie that seemed to cover his face, blue jeans and big black steel toe boots.

Once in the elevator, I stood in the corner directly opposite him, studying him.

There was something so odd about him, and I couldn't place whether it was the fact that I could see none of his face besides his bottom jaw, covered in scruffy beard, or the fact that he seemed almost statuette, not a muscle seemed to move at all.

My sister and mother stepped into the elevator, making their way to the space left beside me. Both of them glanced in his direction as they entered, giving a look of uncertainty.

I almost wondered if this man were too sick, maybe unable to move. Maybe he had just been let out of the fifth floor, where the psychiatric ward had been located, according to the labelling on the buttons. I wasn't sure, but I felt very uneasy.

I watched as my mother reached over and clicked on one of them, the same orange light seemed much brighter from within the little box.

Main floor.

The numbers on the screen above the door began to lower, each floor seeming further and further down, as a butterfly feeling filled my chest.

As I watched the numbers on the screen descend, I noticed something.

There was movement I could see from the corner of my eye. The man.

I glanced back to him, my eyes searching for some trace of humanity, some trace of life.

I watched as his arm lifted, pulling his hood back, only enough that I could make out a nose and jaw.

He wasn't young, but he wasn't old either. My guess would have been that he was probably in his early fifties.

"Elliot?" His voice grumbled, booming through the small space.

I didn't understand and at first I thought that maybe he was only talking to himself, probably stuck inside some sort of psychotic episode, but then I realized that the name was far, far too familiar.

How did he know?

"Wh-What?" I stuttered.

He moved his head into a position that I was sure if I could see his eyes, he would have been glaring directly into mine.

"Last name, Elliot."

No, there was no way he could have known that.

I was almost certain that I had never met this man before in my life.

"How... what?" I couldn't find another word.

"How would you know our last name?" My mom asked him in her most stern, and powerful voice.

Liz remained silent, but I could hear her petrified breathing beside me.

"It's not safe there," he whispered, his voice still bore a growling sound. And then he yelled, "get out, Claire. Get out if you can. Get out. Get out now!"

If I didn't know better, I would say that I watched his mouth unhinge like a snake, as his screams for me to "get out" grew louder, and more terrifying with each word.

As he had finished, I watched as he threw his hood back down over his face, covering what little of him that he had allowed me to see.

There was a *ding,* and the door slid open as he turned away from me, and slipped out of the elevator, disappearing into the crowds of people.

I couldn't move.

How had he known exactly who I was? What did he mean *get out?* Why had those words sent such a pressing cold fear, directly down my spine?

Elizabeth hadn't moved, her breathing was heavy still, but slightly more steady. My mom stood there, staring at the exit of the elevator. I couldn't tell what emotions filled her head, but it seemed something close to fear or anger. Maybe she had known this man?

I suddenly got the feeling that something terrible was erupting.

8

As I stood underneath the large awning just outside the main doors, I found myself glancing behind my shoulders. I was scanning the parking lot, the sidewalks, every inch of the property within my view. I wanted to know who that man was, I needed to know if he was following us, but he was nowhere in sight.

I waited for the taxi to arrive, hiding beneath the awning to shield myself from the rain.

Ping, click. Ping, click.

The sound was almost soothing, as raindrops fell upon the large metal sheet just above my head. The sky was a gloomy grey, dark blue clouds scattered themselves around, creating the illusion of a coming storm.

Elizabeth and my mom sat on the bench behind me.

Liz played on her phone, as my mother checked her watch for the time, repeatedly.

"Did you know that guy?" I found myself asking my mother, as I felt doubt rise within me.

My eyes darted to the hospital doors, and then back to hers as if to say *the guy from the elevator.*

Her eyes adjusted, and grew slightly wider as she stared into mine, seriousness in her tone.

"Of course not."

I wanted to believe her, but I couldn't help but wonder where the truth did lie. How had he known so much? How the hell did he know anything at all?

It just didn't add up.

"Okay," I stated, not one hundred percent convinced.

My eyes turned away from hers, and out to the parking lot, as the sound of a car engine grew nearer.

A yellow and blue ford fusion sat idling just in front of me. I could see the driver through the car window, fumbling with the nobs on the car radio.

He was a very young man, younger looking than me. I wondered if he had even been old enough to drive.

His face looked as though it had never seen a strand of hair. A set of glasses overtook the majority of his face which was probably the reason that it seemed so odd he'd be behind the wheel of a cab. His hair was gelled over into a messy come over, strands of hair escaped his once clean hair do.

Great. As if I wasn't already terrified of getting into a vehicle, now this.

I bit my tongue, trying my best not to make a fuss about it.

Glancing back to my mother and Liz, I could see them standing up from the bench, purses in tow.

"Ready, girls?" My mother asked, her voice as chipper as a child in an amusement park.

Liz shook her head, rolling her eyes, as she walked past my mom.

"Let's just get this over with," I could hear her mumble.

It wouldn't have been easy to admit, but I was actually excited. I was beginning to look forward to the new place, and to be honest, anywhere was better than the hospital.

I smiled halfheartedly, assuring my mom that I wasn't completely dreading it anymore, but I chose not to speak.

There just wasn't anything that I could think to say.

Was I ready to leave here? Hell yeah. Was I ready for a whole new house? A whole new town, if there even was one? A new school, new friends? Not exactly. Was I ready to get into that car? Absolutely not.

9

My mother stepped passed me, and opened the side door to the car.

Liz had walked around the vehicle, making her way to the passenger side. I could see her climb into the car, sitting down in the seat and closing the door behind her.

I scanned the interior, looking for... well I didn't even know. Something strange maybe? Something faulty?

As my eyes studied the stained grey bench seats, the dried mud that had spread itself across the floor, I felt a chill go down my spine.

There wasn't anything visibly wrong with the car, besides maybe the messiness. No. This was something else.

I didn't feel right. My stomach churned, as I tried to figure out what was wrong.

I began to feel as though I was being watched, being followed. I could feel eyes on the back of my head, burning into me as if to say, *I'm here.* I could feel goosebumps beginning to form on the skin beneath my hoodie, my eyes began to water.

Do I dare turn around?

As if something had forced me, I slowly turned my head.

I could see the bench behind me, the bricks that made up the hospital. I could see flower pots filled with daisies, sulking in the cool, wet weather.

I could see the puddles forming on the sidewalk, raindrops rippled within them.

But it wasn't any of that that I had been searching for. No, it was the dark figure standing outside the door, facing right at me.

His hands were the only skin that showed, aside from the jawline that I had seen not long before.

His hands were white, clammy even. A hood was draped over his face, just as it had been before.

His presence was overwhelming.

I felt my eyes grow wide in horror, my hands clenched into fists, reminding me of my broken arm. I loosened my grip.

As I found myself staring back at him, a hand settled on my shoulder, startling me and causing me to jump.

"C'mon, Claire." It was my mother. "Get in the car. Now."

She must have noticed who I had been staring at, because I could hear the shakiness in her voice.

As I attempted to turn around, something stopped me.

I watched as he stepped forward. And then again, and again.

There was something inhuman just in the way he moved. His body moved up and down, as he took long strides, his hands remaining lowered at his sides.

He was moving so quickly, that I wondered if I would have even had time to turn and get into the car.

He was coming, and I was sure that this time he, wasn't going to let me leave.

What do you want? Stop following me! But my words came out much harsher than my thoughts.

"Stop following me!" I screamed. "What the *Fuck* do you want?!"

I could hear my own voice echoing throughout the lot, bouncing straight back to my ears.

He kept coming, just as though he hadn't heard me. There was no way he hadn't.

He was only steps away from the car, when I felt the hand on my shoulder pull, jolting me back and causing me to stumble into the car.

My arm hit the driver's seat as I fell in, though the cloth material cushioned the blow.

I forced myself to sit up as quickly as I could, and moved further into the car, making room for my mom.

I could see him approaching. He seemed to grow larger, and larger with each step.

"Wake up, Claire! Wake up, little girl! You need to get out of the car!" His voice was loud, and immensely terrifying.

What?

"I'm not getting out! Mom, get in the car!"

Just as I had attempted to reach a hand out for my mom, she jumped into the car beside me, slamming the door beside her.

The man didn't retreat.

I watched in horror out the window, as he approached, reaching a hand outwards.

"Lock it, Lock it!" Liz screamed out, her terrified voice filled the interior of the vehicle.

My mother locked the door, as I heard his hand connect with the handle just outside.

I could hear the sound of metal clicking against metal, as he repeatedly tried to open it.

"You're gonna die, Claire!"

I closed my eyes, and threw my hands up to my ears, trying not to let the panic win. My hands were trembling as I struggled not to look, trying to pretend that this wasn't happening.

"Come on, drive!" My mom shouted from beside me, setting an arm around my shoulder, and pulling me in for a protective hug.

Within seconds, I began to feel the car move, and then I heard a thud come from just outside my mother's door.

I forced myself to look up quickly, glancing outside the window. I could see the brick that belonged to the building, windows upon windows as we drove by.

I peered through the rear window to see if he was still there, and to my horror, I could see him standing there.

He remained on the sidewalk, still looking towards the car. He was staring at me again, well, if I could have seen his eyes that's what I would have assumed.

He didn't move at all as the car drove further and further away, leaving him behind in the distance.

Was he going to follow me? Or had he finally given up?

The only reassurance that I had, was that there was no way he could have known where we were going. *Or was there?*

10

"Sorry about that," the cab driver said timidly. "Someone you know?"

I had almost forgot that I was still staring out the back window, his words almost made me jump.

We exited the lot of the hospital, making our way out onto the road.

I turned back to face the front of the car. I didn't know what to respond, and I was thankful that Liz had instead.

"Not one bit. Some fucking creep."

I was surprised to feel Elizabeth's hand fall upon my shoulder, as I looked up to see her face.

There was concern where I hadn't seen it in years.

I smiled an unsure smile, as I rested my head onto her hand.

Did I have my sister back?

"Oh, sorry. If I had known, I'd have left sooner," the driver's voice was high, almost exactly how I had pictured it would sound.

There was a bit of awkward silence, as no one said another word.

What did he mean I was going to die? Was he threatening me? Was he warning me about something?

One thing that I was sure of, I was glad we were going home.

"It's just that I could call the police for you if..."

The driver spoke again, but this time my mom stopped him.

"Okay, can we just have a quiet ride? I just want to get home and not talk, okay? Alright."

It was very rare to hear her speak like that. She was generally a very easy going, kind person.

"Alright, sorry."

I felt bad. He had only been trying to help, but I was sure that my mother hadn't intended to be so rude. After experiencing something like what had just happened, I completely understood why she didn't yearn to involve herself in conversation. But at the same time, I wondered if involving the police might have been the best idea I heard all day.

* * *

The rest of the drive was silent and boring. There was little to nothing to see since we had left Worcester, trees and empty fields were the only things my eyes could find.

I peered out through the window as the car slowed down and pulled into the end of a driveway.

There was a thick, brass gate that stood in front of us, a large K incorporated into it's design.

Must mean something from the previous owners.

On either side of the gate sat a life-size, stone lion. Something about their completely realistic look made me feel uneasy.

I studied them as their eyes seemed to come to life, daring me to cross their path, threatening me to intrude. Their mouths were wide open, as if they were starving, waiting for a soul to devour. Their eyes were heavy and black, like endless holes leading to nowhere at all.

I forced myself to look somewhere else, trying to erase the disturbing feeling that crawled beneath my skin.

I studied the trees, attempting to see the house, but to no avail. Between the trees laid only darkness, emptiness that beckoned me to enter.

"Oh, one second. I have the remote," my mom's voice startled me as I felt her hand graze the side of my thigh.

She was reaching into her pocket, fumbling around for something, a hopeful look spreading across her face.

"I know it's in here somewhere."

I could hear the rattling of keys among other items as her hand pressed into my leg, and then her face lit up in satisfaction.

"Got it!" She announced. "Do you mind driving us up to the house? It's just a couple acres into the path there."

She spoke to the driver as she pulled a small black square from her pocket.

My mother lifted the remote up, pointing it towards the gate. She clicked the only button on the controller, and it was followed by a loud eerie sound.

Even from inside the car, with all of the windows up, I could hear the oil thirsty gate squeal. A heavy vibration accompanied as it opened up, welcoming us with unsure pleasure.

I thought about what the man had said.

Get out. You're going to die, Claire.

His words echoed inside my head. If only I knew what he had meant.

The gate finished opening with a loud *boom.* I could see the metal bars shaking as it came to a halt. The sound echoed throughout the trees as I watched a few shadows of birds fly up from their branches.

"Sure, I'll bring ya up to the house."

The cab driver was hesitant. I knew that it was not in his best interests to be driving down a long, dark path in the middle of the night. He was most likely just trying to be kind, as he could have just forced us all to walk from there.

He slowly hit the gas pedal, forcing us into the driveway, and as we entered, I swore I could see someone standing between two of the trees.

11

I squinted my eyes, attempting to adjust them to the darkness, inching my head forward as I tried to study the figure. It was shaped like a person, but was completely still, blending into shadows and trees.

What is that?

My mother must have noticed that I had been staring so concernedly, because I could see her from the corner of my eye, attempting to follow my gaze.

The car drove slowly as I studied the shadow, trying to make sense of it. I wanted to believe that it was just a small tree or something, but I had to be sure.

"This place is creepy," Liz stated, her voice more matter of fact than scared.

I glanced away from the window to look at my sister who had been staring out hers.

"Did you see something?" I asked, fear rising noticeably in me.

"No. It just gives me the creeps."

I nodded, even though she hadn't been looking at me, and turned my head back to my window, searching again for the shadow.

That's weird.

I shivered.

It's gone.

My eyes began to water, as I felt the urge to run away, to run back to Portland and hide in my room. But I knew that it wasn't an option. I had no home there anymore.

I continued to study the trees, trying to find any shape at all that could have resembled what I had been looking at, and still, there was nothing.

"What were you looking at, Claire?" My mom asked, still peering out the window to where I had been looking.

I turned my eyes to her as I noticed the confused expression on her face. She was biting her lip, her eyebrows tensed, as she turned back to me.

"Never mind," I stated, attempting to remove the vision from my mind. "It was probably nothing."

It was only about a two or three minute drive from the road to the house. The darkness seemed endless as we made our way down the long, empty driveway, trees stretched across either side of it.

And then, finally, I could see the house.

It wasn't at all what I would have expected, taking into consideration the expensive looking gate at the road.

The house was large, but... regular. What I had expected to see as a gigantic Victorian style mansion, was actually an old brick house, nothing too fancy.

There was a bed of what must have previously been a garden sitting just outside the side door, weeds grew throughout, spilling outside. There were two lamps on either side of the door, both were lit up but very dull. There was a large porch at the back door to the house, that almost wrapped around the whole place.

The railing was made up of broken wood, pieces scattered across the lawn in front of it. A small lantern sat on the porch table.

The grass looked as if it hadn't been cut in months, long weeds as tall as me covered what must have been the back lawn.

In the middle of the weeds I could make out some sort of brick, something circular. What was it?

"That's the well," my mom stated, as I noticed that she had been looking at me. "I'm gonna cover it up, so just don't go near it for now, okay? I don't need something else happening."

I nodded.

Was she afraid that my sister and I would get into a fight, one pushing the other one over? I couldn't help but think that maybe it was something else entirely.

I was startled as the car suddenly stopped.

"Alright, you guys are good to go."

I gulped, as I turned to Liz, who had been silently staring at the house, too.

"Here goes nothing," I mumbled under my breath, as I adjusted myself in my seat.

The sound of items and purses shuffling filled the car as Liz and my mother gathered their things.

"Where's my things, Mom?" I asked, turning to her, suddenly realizing that I hadn't had my bag since the accident.

She pulled her wallet from her purse and reached in for her credit card, looking at me as she slid it out.

"It's in your room. I went to the impound and got all of our stuff out of the car and already dropped it off, that's why I was here earlier. We moved some things here from the moving truck, too, but they're coming back tomorrow to bring the rest."

I hadn't even thought of the car, or any of our things from home.

"Okay. Need help tomorrow?" I offered, knowing full-well that I wouldn't be much help.

She rolled her eyes and shook her head.

"No, that's okay. Liz can help me."

I glanced over to my sister just in time to see her make a ridiculous face at my mother, and then return to her normal expression.

I pretended not to notice, turning back to face my mom.

I waited as she used the debit machine that the driver had handed her, her fingers moving fast as she finished punching in numbers. She pulled her card out quickly and handed the machine back to the driver.

My mother dropped her card into a large pocket in her purse, not seeming to care much for where it would land.

She hesitated for a minute before opening the car door.

"Thank you for bringing us all this way, none of the other companies were willing to send anyone this far."

I could see the cab driver nod through the rear-view mirror, a polite smile took over his lips.

My mother pulled the handle and forced the door open, picking up her purse and climbing out of the car. Liz did the same.

I hesitated before getting out, unsure of why.

Something was telling me to stay in the car. Something was telling me not to get out.

The feeling was overwhelming, but it was as if something horrific was going to happen if I did. But I knew that I didn't have a choice.

"Be careful getting back to the city," I wasn't sure exactly what I wanted to warn him about, but I felt that I had to at least say something. "It's really dark."

I was looking at him through the mirror again, his expression was slightly less professionally uptight, and a little bit more fearful and worried.

I wondered if he would be okay. I began to picture the shadow, coming back, coming for... but I pushed those thoughts away.

This was my first night in this house. I wasn't willing to spend the entire night, laying awake in fear, thinking of the worst. After everything that had happened that day, what I really needed was a good night's sleep.

"Come on, Claire! I'm tired!" Liz whined from the other side of the car door, and I realized that I was holding both of them up.

"Coming!"

I slid myself down the bench seat and basically jumped out of the car. Rocks slid across each other as my feet fell to the drive.

My legs weren't really that sore anymore, and I could barely feel the cuts on my face. My arm was the only thing that was still giving me trouble, but even that felt a little bit better since leaving the hospital.

I turned and closed the door behind me, the *thud* echoed throughout the trees and into the empty yard.

I looked up to the house, as the car inched forwards and performed a three-point turn.

I didn't bother to look back as I heard the vehicle drive past us, the sound of the engine disappearing into the long, dark driveway.

I tried to ignore the goosebumps that were beginning to form all over my body. Were they caused by the chill of the late fall night? Or maybe it was the feeling that ran through me, as a small gust of wind blew through my hair.

It was silent. There were no sounds of crickets chirping in the distant night, no traces of birds singing within the trees. Not even the shuffling of leaves were present, as I thought almost certainly, that there would be wild animals scouring about.

The pattering of footsteps against creaky wood suddenly echoed off into the yard. I looked up to see that my mother and Liz were already up on the porch, making their way to the door.

I began to feel a presence that I couldn't quite describe. It was a similar feeling to what I had experienced back at the hospital, but not exactly the same.

It felt as though the trees were watching me, the house daring me to enter.

I could see only darkness within the windows of the house, and it suddenly didn't feel so inviting.

A shiver ran down my spine as I realized that I was still standing in the driveway, completely alone.

Something isn't right.

I started towards the porch, glancing to the long narrow drive that we had come down. I thought of the shadow that I had laid eyes on only minutes ago, the one that had been watching me. The one that I felt had been warning me to turn around, and I began to wish that I would have listened.

I almost expected to see it again, standing in the middle of the gravel, or off to the side attempting to blend in with the trees. But, there was nothing there.

The branches swayed with the cool wind of the night, a few leaves breaking free and falling down to the rocks with elegance.

I looked up to the porch again as I made my way closer, forcing myself to move more quickly.

I could hear my mother fumbling through her key ring.

"Are you good, Claire? Need any help up the stairs?" I could hear metal scraping against metal as the key turned the lock free.

I stumbled up the stairs slowly, my arm resting against the unsteady banister, as it threatened to fall apart against my weight.

"No, it's okay Mom... I got it," Truth be told, I probably could have used a little bit of help, but I was one to rarely admit that. "I'm not broken."

As I neared the top of the stairs, I could see my mom standing there with the door wide open, Elizabeth nowhere in sight.

She must already be inside.

The wood boards creaked beneath my feet, as I feared they might crack, and snap, beneath my weight.

My mom reached an arm out for me, setting one gently onto my shoulder, as if trying to force me inside.

I stepped inside to find that we were in the kitchen. It had looked identical to the photos, everything right down to the beautiful chandelier was exactly the same.

I noticed that a few of our appliances were scattered across the counter, boxes of non-perishable food sat upon the table.

The door closed behind me as I studied the room.

There was a sort of elegance that didn't match. It was such a beautiful room, so why had the feeling of such a sinister presence lay within it's walls?

I tried to ignore it. I tried to ignore myself, pleading from the inside to just get out of that house. I couldn't just leave, it just wasn't that simple.

"Where did Elizabeth go?" I asked, my eyes scanning around for her.

There was a hallway that led to the rest of the house just beside me. A light was on somewhere else in the house, but the hall itself stood in darkness.

I could hear the moving of boxes, footsteps echoing in through the hall. Was it Liz?

Just as I had began to convince myself that it was just my sister moving things, something happened. A sound carried through the house, echoing off of every wall and corner, seeming so much closer to me than it must have been.

A shrill, blood-curdling scream made it's way through the hallway and filled my ears. It was Elizabeth.

12

Before I could even think to move, my mom ran past me, bolting down the hallway and disappearing into the house.

The screams continued.

I gathered my strength and ran after her, my heart beating out of my chest.

The hall was longer than I had expected. There were three closed doors sitting parallel from each other, and an open doorway at the end.

I could see my mother, climbing quickly up the staircase that started only a few feet ahead of me. She was running so fast that I had barely seen her for two seconds, as she disappeared onto the next floor.

As I stepped onto the stairs, my stomach felt weak.

No... Elizabeth. The shadow. The house.

Chilling thoughts tried to weasel their way in, as I fought to push them back down.

No. I can't think like that. She's fine.

My legs seemed non-existent, as I ran as fast as I could up the stairs.

I followed the sounds of her screams, listening closely to where they had been coming from.

Is she okay? No, Liz. No.

Once at the top of the stairs, I could see a silhouette of a woman entering into a doorway.

There was only a small landing at the top, with what looked to be three or four bedrooms and a bathroom.

I couldn't tell which one of the rooms Liz's screams were coming from, but I decided to follow my mother.

I ran across the hardwood, quickly entering the room to my right.

I bolted in, before I could even think, and I couldn't believe my eyes.

It was dark.

Too dark.

As I stared in astonishment the screaming subsided, and I realized that it had, in fact, been coming from behind me.

What the hell?

I couldn't bring myself to turn away. Was my mother in here? Surely it must have been her that I watched turn the corner. But it didn't make any sense.

"Claire," I heard a voice behind me, as the lights flickered on.

I could see a huge queen size bed, the comforters set neatly on top, not a corner set out of place. Beneath a window, sat a white dresser, carvings of leaves and flowers outlined the trim, a large vanity mirror sat just on top. Curtains as red as wine hung across the walls, covering what seemed to be dozens of french windows.

There were a few boxes piled up against the wall beside me, and I realized that my mother must have already brought a few things up.

There was no sign of anyone inside.

What is going on?

"Claire," the voice behind me whispered again, and I turned around to find that it was my mom. "Honey, what are you doing in here?"

I hesitated.

"I saw you..." I stopped. There was a puzzled expression on her face.

I didn't want to seem as though I were going crazy on the first night, and I already knew what she would have said if I told her what I saw. *It's a new place, you're going to be uneasy, but you'll get used to it.* It just didn't seem worth it.

"Nothing, mom. Never mind. Is Liz okay?"

Relief swept over me as I realized that she didn't seem worried anymore. Whatever had happened was probably nowhere near what I had pictured.

"She's fine. I just have a mess to clean," she replied. "Do you like my bedroom?"

What did she mean a mess? It wasn't like Liz to scream over something as simple as spilt milk.

"Yeah... it's nice."

I really wasn't sure about the room. It was a lovely bedroom itself, but after what I had seen, I wasn't sure that I ever wanted to go back inside.

I followed my mom back out of the bedroom, flicking the light off behind me.

"Where's Liz?" I asked, although I was sure she must have been inside one of the other two rooms.

She pointed a finger in the direction of the door that sat just across from her new room.

"That one's hers."

I stared at the door for a moment, not even bothering to move. Did I even want to see what was in there?

I inched forward and grasped the handle, turning it slightly and pushing the door open with my shoulder.

"Liz," I called, my voice nearly a whisper, as I pressed the door open. A lingering *creak* filled the emptiness behind me, as I tried to focus my eyes inside the room.

I could see Liz, sitting on the edge of her bed as she scrolled through her phone quickly. She was pressing down on the screen over and over, then lifting it to her ear. When she would pull it away, I would only see her do the same thing over again.

She didn't answer.

She didn't even look at me as I entered the room.

"Liz, everything okay?" I asked again, more hopeful for an answer this time.

Her eyes darted up to me, wide in fear. It was a look on her that I had never seen before, and it sent a chilling shiver across my body.

"Li-."

"The phone's won't work. The phone's won't work, I don't want to be here. I don't like this place, Claire. I can't be here," she cut me off, her voice was shaken.

I swore that in that moment, I felt exactly what she had felt. I knew exactly what she meant. There was something wrong with the house, something that didn't make any sense. But I wouldn't let her know.

If she found out that her big sister, too, was as frightened as she was, I was sure that she would lose it.

"It's just a phone, Elizabeth," was all I could say, and I wondered if my phone would work either.

The house was in the middle of practically nowhere, so the idea that we would have horrible reception wasn't really far-fetched.

"Oh. Yeah, you're right," her words were full of sarcasm. "But why don't you tell that to the dead cat inside my closet!"

Her hand rose up, phone still stuck within her grasp, as she pointed a finger to just beside me.

I turned to see a wooden door standing partially open. I was about to look, but decided not to, since my chances of getting sleep that night were already slim.

"It's okay, Liz. It's gonna be fine. We'll try to figure the phones out in the morning."

I wasn't really sure what to say about the cat, since I knew that if I had seen it, I would have probably been losing my mind too.

Footsteps approached behind me, as I turned to see my mother carrying in a small white garbage bag.

"You don't want to see this," she warned, as she stepped past me towards the closet.

She was right, *I didn't.*

I waited as she pried the closet door open and leaned in. I could hear her bagging up the body, and it felt as if we were trying to hide some kind of crime scene.

It seemed to take forever, but finally, she backed away from the closet. The bag she held was no longer weightless and flat. There was a dark bulge that now sat at the bottom of the bag, and I could make out strands of fur within it.

"Poor kitty, must have got stuck in there," my mom said, as she turned again towards the door. "I'm gonna go get rid of this, you girls should try to get some sleep. It's nearly two in the morning."

Liz dropped her cell phone to the floor purposely, seeming to give up hope on it for the night.

I yawned.

I was tired, but it wasn't until my mother said those words that I realized *how tired.*

"Yeah," I replied, turning towards the door behind her. "I'm gonna try to get some sleep."

"Night," Liz stated, as she laid across her bed, not bothering to cover herself up.

"Call for me if you need anything," I told her.

She didn't move or say anything else as my mother and I left the room.

We walked down the stairs and headed back for the hallway that had led to the kitchen.

"Where's my room supposed to be?"

She stopped right in front of me, almost causing me to walk right into her.

I couldn't help but allow my eyes to lock onto the bag within her grasp, swinging gently, back and forth.

How could she have just walked around so casually with something like that? Like it was a pile of laundry... like it was a sac of potatoes?

"Oh, right. I nearly forgot! You're room is here off the hall. Right there on your right. We already moved your bed and stuff in."

I hesitated.

"Thanks, mom," I let out another yawn. "I'll see you in the morning?"

I asked as if there was a chance that I wouldn't.

"Love you," was all she said as she continued, disappearing into the kitchen.

I pushed the door open to my room, peering inside. Dark.

I placed my hand up against the wall beside the doorway, feeling around for a light switch.

There's gotta be one here.

The light from the hallway lit up just enough that I could make out the foot of my bed, my comforters from home set neatly over it.

I swiped my hand back and forth against the wall until I found that my entire arm was searching for it.

What was that?

As my arm grew further into the room, my fingers hit something, nearly knocking it over. I put my hand out to steady the object, cold glass pressed against my fingertips.

Just as I was about to call for my mother to come help me locate it, my elbow brushed against something. Something plastic and square, one little knob sticking out from it. The light switch.

As I flicked my finger against it, the room lit up.

My bed and my dresser were already there, placed neatly inside the room. Boxes labelled 'Claire's things' were piled up in the far corner of the room. My purse sat upon my desk next to the only window within the room, my phone sat beside it.

I looked beside me to see my lamp sitting on an end table, and was relieved that I hadn't let it fall.

Exhausted, I clicked on my lamp and turned off the main light to the bedroom.

I usually liked to sleep in the dark, but on this particular night, there was no way that I would have slept.

I left my bedroom door open as I made my way to the bed.

Flopping down as if I were weightless, I fumbled with the covers and laid my head down on my pillow.

I rested my eyes, and before I knew it, I must have fallen asleep.

13

I was awoken by the sound of raindrops pelting against glass, thunder booming in the distance.

Thunderstorms were one of those things that always had a way of calming me, relaxing me regardless of what mood I was in.

I remembered how my father and I would sit outside on our deck, staring up into the sky, watching the clouds pass. Those nights were some of my most fondest childhood memories with him. He had never really been home much, even then, but whenever we had had the chance, we were always sure to watch them together.

There was a night when Liz and I had gotten into an argument over something ridiculous, I had ran and hid away inside my bedroom. I remember my father knocking on the door.

"Claire, come sit outside," he had said. "I've got hot chocolate."

Being only ten, the sound of marshmallows and chocolatey bliss was something I just couldn't resist.

We had gone outside, sat on the front porch and sipped at our hot cocoa. Neither of us had said a word, as we stared up into the grey sky, raindrops falling all around us.

Somehow, the rain here seemed strange. With it came an ominous feeling, an eerie presence that spread it's way along the property, blanketing the house that I had yet to call my home.

A cold shiver made me realize how chilly the room had become. I grasped my comforter and pulled it up to my chin, unwilling to allow any heat to escape from beneath it.

I laid there for a few minutes, eyes closed, attempting to fall back asleep.

Yeah, right.

Not long after, I had given up.

Wondering what time it was, I turned and reached for my phone. As I picked it up from the table, I clicked the side button, the light from the screen illuminated the walls around me.

Seven o'clock.

When I noticed that I hadn't received any text notifications, I swiped up on the screen.

Weird.

I hadn't checked my phone since before the accident and somehow, I didn't receive a single text or phone call.

I stared at the screen in astonishment, my eyes still trying to adjust. *Had everyone cared so little? Had Carissa forgotten about me already? Was she angry with me?*

As I filled my own head with useless scenarios, I noticed something in the top right hand corner.

NO SERVICE.

I suddenly remembered what Elizabeth had been saying the night before.

The phone won't work.

So now what? We were in the middle of nowhere. No phones, no car, no way of even contacting the outside world.

I was beginning to feel sick to my stomach.

Tossing the covers, I decided to go check to see if Liz was up yet. I knew that with no phone, her of all people, would be losing her mind.

As I stood up, a sharp pain in my arm almost caused me to fall back over.

"Ow!" I found myself shouting out loud.

I looked down to my arm, as if to see anything other than a cast, but nothing had changed.

Convincing myself that it had only been the way I had slept, I carried on to the hallway, clicking off the lamp on the way out.

Thunder seemed to echo throughout the empty hall as I passed through, heading for Liz's bedroom. My feet were the only audible sound that lingered, as I made my way up the staircase.

I first peeked into my mother's room. Peering in through the doorway, I could make out a large lump underneath the covers. It moved with the rhythm of her breath as I realized that she was still sound asleep.

Turning away from the doorway, I slid down to my sister's room.

I peered into the dark room, studying the bed that laid directly across from the doorway.

I could see blankets strewn across the bed, and falling lazily to the floor. There was no formation beneath the covers as there had been in my mother's room.

Most of the dresser drawers were pulled halfway out, clothes spilling out from inside of them. I could see her cell phone settled on top, a set of keys beside it.

There was no sign of Elizabeth.

14

I began to panic, as I wondered where she could be. Surely, I would have heard her walking around, had she been awake before me.

I remembered how uneasy she had felt about the house when we had first arrived, how she had screamed when she had found the body of a cat laying in her closet. I thought of how she had been so upset when she discovered that her phone wasn't retaining any signal.

Doubt filled my mind as I convinced myself more and more, that she wouldn't have gone exploring by herself.

What about what I had seen the night before? Had something terrible happened to her?

No.

I pushed those horrible thoughts away from my imagination, as I tried to bury the memory of what I had seen.

I couldn't be weak. I had to stop, and force myself to be strong.

I unglued my eyes from her empty room, and turned back towards the stairs.

I wanted to shout and call her name. I wanted to yell and tell her to stop playing. I wanted to find her and give her a good old high-five to the head for making me worry.

I tip-toed as silently as I could manage down the hardwood stairs, listening for her footsteps, her voice.

"Liz," I whispered, almost no sound at all escaping my mouth.

There was no response.

Once at the bottom of the stairs, I whispered again, louder this time.

"Elizabeth."

Hoping that this was all a big joke, I walked through the hall, passing by my bedroom and making my way to the kitchen.

There was a small plate sitting on the counter, a mess of toast crumbs left behind. I didn't notice that there when I had gone to bed the previous night, my nerves began to settle, only slightly.

She must have made herself breakfast.

I was about to turn around and head downstairs to check the living room, when I noticed something just outside the kitchen window.

What the hell was that?

It resembled something like that of a cloud. Smoke maybe?

Was there a fire brewing outside?

I darted over to the kitchen door, turning the handle and pushing the door open.

I instantly noticed that horrible smell filling my nostrils. The smell of chemicals mixed with God knows what almost caused me to choke, as I turned around to see Liz sitting on the porch.

"Please, don't tell mom!" She shrieked, as I watched her press a cigarette butt into the old, crumbling wood of the porch. "I thought you were sleeping!"

Mixed feelings of relief and anger washed over me as I stared at her in disbelief.

You're thirteen years old! I wanted to scream at her. *What the hell do you think you're doing?*

I might have lost control that day if I hadn't, only seconds before, been so unbelievably worried.

Part of me wanted to turn around, march back upstairs and tell my mother. The other part of me knew that there was nothing she would be able to do. This couldn't have been the first time Elizabeth had done this, and the only thing that telling on her would accomplish, would be to make her hate me again. I wasn't exactly willing to go back there again. Not now.

I knew that I was all she had there, apart from my mom. She wouldn't be able to sit around texting her friends all day like she had done in Portland, and I needed to be there for her.

The more I thought about it, the more I realized that just maybe, I needed her even more than she needed me.

"Please don't tell," she begged, looking up at me with wide-open, pleading eyes.

I bit my lip.

"I won't tell her. But I wish you wouldn't do it."

She looked down, her eyes landing on a cracked board that was barely even intact.

I began to wonder if that was the only thing she had done. I could only hope that she hadn't done anything worse, but in all honesty, I didn't really want to know.

"Thank you," she mumbled, looking back up to me.

She picked herself up off the ground slowly, taking a step toward me.

"Is she still sleeping?"

A look of caution filled her eyes as she peered into the doorway behind me.

"I think so," I answered, glancing back into the house, myself.

I placed my hand on my cast as an unforgiving itch formed beneath it. I forced a finger between plaster and skin, moving it just enough that it was bearable again.

"That thing must be annoying," she said, rolling her eyes and staring at my cast. "When's it come off again?"

I couldn't remember. They said a few weeks, but how long was that supposed to be?

"I'm not sure.." I responded, inching my way back into the house. "Hopefully soon."

We made our way into the kitchen, Liz closing the door behind her.

My eyes fixed on the empty plate that sat on the counter, as I tried to think of a better way to start the day.

"I'm gonna go take a quick shower, Liz, maybe we can check out the rest of the house after?"

I really didn't want to walk around outside in the rain, but I figured we could at least look around and tour the rooms in the house.

As much as the house had made me feel uneasy, there really wasn't much else to do, and I thought that maybe it was something we could do together.

"Yeah, sure," she agreed, picking up the plate and setting it into the sink beside it. "I'll go unpack for now. Lemme know when you're done."

I nodded, and then I headed down the hall.

The bathroom was clean and spacious. There was a decent size tub, and a shower that looked as if it were much newer than the rest of the house.

A large mirror took up almost the entirety of the wall just above the double sinks. The walls were made up of tile, a dark hunters green reflected off the mirror and throughout the room. It was one of the biggest bathrooms that I had ever seen other than in a public establishment.

I set my towel down on the counter, and studied my face in the mirror.

The scabs that were once gashes were sealed up tight with wire stitches. My nose was scraped, eyes, a deep shade of purple. I could barely recognize the person looking back at me.

Finding myself unappealing, I turned away from the mirror and headed to the shower.

I opened the glass door to find that the inside of the shower was made up of the identical porcelain tiles as the rest of the room.

I tossed my clothes into the hamper and stepped inside, the tile cold against the soles of my feet.

I turned the tap on, allowing warm water to fall into my hair and eventually the rest of me.

The water droplets coated my skin, creating a blanket of warmth that made me feel almost instantly more awake. And, for the first time since being in that house, I felt calm.

Closing my eyes, I ran my fingers through my hair, allowing the droplets to hit every spot of my head.

I opened my eyes, still sifting water throughout my hair, and as I went to turn around, I froze in fear.

15

"Liz?" I whispered, staring at the glass door of the shower.

No reply.

"Mom?"

Still nothing.

I began to feel claustrophobic, trapped inside the tiny space. There was no way I could get out, and I was too terrified to move.

Through the glass, I could see the silhouette of someone... or something.

I couldn't see a face. I couldn't even make out a body. There was only a dark shape, but I could tell that it was looking directly at me, standing only a few feet away the shower.

It was threatening me, daring me to move, daring me to make a sound.

The sound of the water against the tile suddenly didn't bare such a relaxing feeling.

My eyes began to water as I prayed that it was just Liz, as I hoped that it was just my imagination again.

"Liz?" I whispered, so silently that it was almost as if I'd said nothing at all.

As I stared into the dark shape, I began to wonder if maybe I had thrown my towel into an odd position, making it land in a way that could resemble what I was seeing.

I wondered if maybe there was a coat rack in the centre of the room that I had somehow overlooked, but I knew that wasn't true. No, this was something else.

As I attempted to turn the shadow into something from my imagination, I watched in horror as it turned, and slowly walked away.

What the fuck?

I wanted out of the shower. I wanted to open the door, get out and run. But the bathroom door hadn't opened, or closed.

What if this person, or this thing, was simply waiting in the corner of the room for me to try and get out?

They couldn't have left. The door *didn't open.*

Not a muscle in my body dared to move, as I tried to think of what to do next.

I could just scream and hope someone comes? I could open the door, and run? I could sit in here and wait until someone comes to see if I'm still alive? I could attempt to speak to whatever was in the room with me?

I thought about so many different possible escape plans, but only one seemed possible.

I turned the handle on the tap, causing the water to shut off, the wet blanket of warmth turning to a cold sheet of ice.

I pushed the door open as quickly as I could, and jumped out of the shower, bolting to the counter and picking up my towel.

As I reached the mirror, I noticed one thing that I hadn't expected.

There was no one in the room with me.

I let out a sigh of relief as my nerves began to settle, my muscles relaxed.

Am I going crazy? I wondered. *Was I only seeing things?*

No.

I was certain that what I had seen had, in fact, been just as real as my very own flesh.

Picking up the towel and wrapping it around myself, I glanced behind me. My eyes met the corner of the room to where I was sure that someone would have been standing.

Bare, green rectangular tiles sat across the wall, each one perfectly symmetrical with the next.

I could clearly see that I was alone in the room, but somehow, I couldn't shake the sinister presence that remained.

16

Back in my bedroom, I struggled as I tried to fit my arm through my blue hoodie, guiding the sleeve with my other hand in an attempt to let it through more easily.

I pushed my arm through as hard as I could bare, and slid the fabric back around the cast.

Finally, I forced it through.

Stupid cast. I couldn't wait to have it removed. I was beginning to forget what that arm had felt like without a heavy weight wrapped around it.

Turning towards my bed, I decided to check my phone again.

I walked over and picked it up, not hoping for much.

NO SERVICE.

Frustrated, I tossed it onto my bed. There was something very unsettling that accompanied the thought of having no way to contact anyone beyond the house.

I wanted to call Carissa, to tell her what I had seen.

She had always been a superstitious person, always searching for things she could list as supernatural.

I remembered the day when she had so badly wanted to go and check out an old abandoned house back in the city. There were stories circulating around that it had been haunted, and she dragged me down there with her.

It was the middle of the night. We sneaked out through our bedroom windows and met up. It must have been at least two hours we had spent in there, me begging Car to leave, her, searching for something insane.

I remembered that old boarded up place as if I had been there yesterday. The wood, rotting and falling apart like that of our porch. The creaking that echoed from the floors where no one would step.

I can't say that I didn't believe in the paranormal, I just didn't like to seek it. I had always thought that if something wanted to contact me, it probably would have, and that it would be better to leave things undisturbed.

I opened up the door to my room to find a heavy scent of cooking bacon, the savoury smell travelled from the kitchen down to the hall.

Is mom awake?

I found myself staring into the open doorway to the bathroom as I exited mine, half-expecting someone to be staring back at me.

Small bits of greyish light made it's way into the room, illuminating parts of the wall, turning the green colours of the wall to a much more dull shade.

Thankfully, there was no one there.

I headed into the kitchen, where I could see my mother standing over the stove, spatula in hand.

The room seemed different in the light of the day, bigger, almost.

I stepped over to the window and peered outside, hoping for a visible break in the clouds.

I wanted to go for a walk and escape from the house for a few hours, but I wasn't exactly willing to go out and get sopping wet and cold.

Maybe tomorrow.

Glancing back to my mom, I could see her dropping bread into the toaster and then hustling over the stove again.

"Need any help, mom?" I offered. I would have done just about anything to occupy my thoughts in that moment, to remove from my memory the events that that morning had held.

I wondered if maybe it had all been a big misunderstanding, that maybe my mother had come in to let me know she was making food. I thought that maybe it was Elizabeth, trying her absolute hardest just to freak me out. A prank, maybe?

"Mom, did you..." she spoke over me before I could finish.

"No honey, I got this. You just relax and have a good day today. Check out the house."

There was a hint of dissatisfaction in her voice, and I couldn't understand why. *Did something else happen?*

I wondered if she had seen anything strange, if she had felt anything that wasn't quite right. Was I losing my mind?

She must have realized she had cut me off, because she spoke again.

"What were you going to say, Claire? I'm sorry, I'm having a heck of a morning so far."

I paused, trying to decide if it was worth asking or not. I was fairly certain that it was not her that had been in the bathroom.

"I was just going to... I wanted to know..." I couldn't think of how to ask without sounding like a mental patient. "Were you in the bathroom at all?"

She paused for a moment, and then twisted the nob on the stove, pulling the frying pan off of the burner. As she turned around to face me, I could see that she had an eyebrow raised.

"No," she answered, her tone quite serious. "I use the one attached to my room, upstairs. I haven't been in there yet except to look. Why do you ask?"

There was no point in pretending I hadn't seen anything. I had already let the cat out of the bag.

"Nothing, I just thought I saw someone. Maybe it was Liz."

I knew that wasn't true. I knew that it wasn't her.

My mom's expression immediately changed, and I wondered if she even believed me. Did she think that I was losing it? Did she think that it was some kind of attempt at convincing her to move us back to Portland?

I didn't know, but it really didn't matter. There was no way to change the way the house made me feel, no way to undo what I had seen.

She turned her back to me, as she scooped out bacon from the pan, setting it down onto a plate of napkins.

"What's wrong, mom?" I asked, trying to make sense of her sudden irritation.

She continued transferring food as she answered.

"Nothing, really, Claire. The phone's apparently don't get any service out here, which the Realtor failed to tell me. I can't even make a phone call, what if your dad needs something? I don't even know when he's coming home."

She stopped, setting her hands on either side of her head, and leaning onto the counter.

Home. That wasn't the word that came to mind when I thought of this place. It was a house, but nothing close to home.

"It's okay, mom. I'm sure he'll be home soon."

I walked over to my mother, setting my good arm down on her shoulder.

She lifted her head up, reaching a hand up behind her neck and setting it down on mine.

"Thanks, honey," she sighed, pulling her hand back away. "What are you and your sister going to do today?"

I had almost forgot about the self tour we were going to take of the house, and a part of me wished that I hadn't come up with the *stupid* idea.

It was too late to back out of it now.

"We were planning on looking around the house... what time was the moving truck supposed to be here?"

She was dishing out helpings of eggs and bacon when she paused, the handle of the spatula slamming down on the sleek wooden counter top. I watched as she recomposed herself, continuing to scoop out large portions of food onto different plates.

"I forgot about that, they're coming at ten. What *bloody* time is it?"

She glanced up to the clock that hung high above the sink, nodding in dissatisfaction. I looked up to see that it was 9:45am.

She picked up two plates and walked them over, placing them down gently on the table.

I was just about to go get Elizabeth when I could hear footsteps emerging from around the corner. I looked up to the doorway, and just as I was beginning to think that maybe I was hearing someone else, she walked into the kitchen.

There was a short silence as she paused, standing in the doorway.

"Why are you looking at me like that?" She asked, her tone harsh.

I realized that my mouth was half-hanging open, my eyes wide and my heart was slightly racing.

Was I really that much on edge?

My expression quickly changed, as I realized how dumb I had probably looked.

"Nothing, sorry. I was just about to come get you for breakfast. Mom made eggs."

I couldn't help but feel ridiculous as I turned around and took a seat at the table, Liz followed.

My mother slid a plate over to each of us, and took a seat on the opposite side.

In front of me sat two sunny-side up eggs, a pile of bacon and a slice of golden-brown buttered toast. Everything was made to perfection and I so badly wanted to devour it, but I could only stare.

I found it hard to take a bite as my nerves refused to settle, but I forced myself to pick up my fork.

"So... are you still up for looking around after breakfast?"

Liz's voice caught me off guard, causing me to flinch, nearly dropping my fork back down to the table.

There was a pause and just as I was about to answer, my mom spoke instead.

"You're helping me today, young lady."

Lifting my gaze to my sister, I could see her rolling her eyes, an annoyed look taking over the cheerfulness that had began to form.

17

After lunch, I decided to wait for Elizabeth in my bedroom.

My mother had refused to let me help, no matter how many times the offer had been made. I felt horrible that they would have to unload the truck by themselves, but to be fair, some alone time was probably long overdue. I felt as though since the accident, I had been completely surrounded, smothered, even.

I pulled my old sketchbook from one of the boxes that I'd packed away, setting it gently down onto my desk. Just as I was about to pull a chair out and take a seat, I noticed the door that sat across from me. It was located on the same side of the wall as the doorway, and I wondered how big the closet could be. Surely, it couldn't have been that big. The hallway sat just on the other side of the door, not allowing for much space in between.

Curious, I made my way over to what I believed would be a tiny closet. Placing my hand around the door handle, I turned the metal knob and attempted to pull it open.

That's odd.

The door wouldn't budge.

I twisted the handle again, harder this time and gave it a hearty tug. It still wouldn't open.

I studied the door, my eyes searching for anything that could point to an answer.

My fingers grazed something as I felt around and underneath the door handle, something circular in shape, something hollow.

A keyhole.

I paused for a moment, and then glanced around the room, as if I expected to see a random key sitting against the hardwood floor.

Just as I had suspected, there was nothing.

I thought about going to ask my mother if she knew anything about the door, if maybe she had been given a key for it. Hesitating, I decided to ask her after they were done unpacking.

Giving up on the door, I pulled out the chair that sat in front of my desk and took a seat, flipping my notebook open to a blank sheet of paper.

I began to draw in what resembled the city of Portland, tracing back and forth as the jagged lines I created came to life.

I was never a self-conceited person, but I liked to think that my drawings turned out quite nicely, for the most part.

* * *

Hours must have passed as I became lost within my work.

I was nearly finished when I set my pencil down and studied my creation, nit-picking the small lines that had darted out of place.

The replication of my old high school was almost exact, the houses surrounding it gave it a feeling of home. The flower beds surrounding the front of the building were exactly as I had remembered them being. The dark shading of the windows sent out a vibe of vacancy, loneliness.

I began to wish that I was back there, in the city that I had referred to as my home.

Wishing that it were possible to just step into the piece of paper, I pictured myself standing there, from the view that it had been drawn.

I longed to walk through the empty, after hours halls of that place.

I remembered Carissa and I, walking through those quiet halls after school had been let out for the day. She had gone there to speak with one of her teachers about a bad grade she had received. On that day, we spent a lot of time messing around by the lockers. At one point, we had joked about hiding out inside one of the lockers and jumping out to scare the janitor. It was an idea that hadn't taken place, but the very thought had made us burst out into laughter.

Becoming lost into my artwork, memories of the past flooded through me. The good times, the bad times... times that I could never get back.

The feeling of a presence fell upon me, as I snapped back into reality. It was a strange feeling, but it didn't feel as horrible as the last time I had felt it, back at the hospital.

Before the feeling could settle, I didn't even have time to turn and look, as someone spoke.

"Mom said we're done for the day. I have to help unpack some boxes tomorrow but everything's offloaded."

It was Liz.

I exhaled a long breath of air, as I realized who it was behind me, and turned to face her.

I found myself staring into her eyes as I remembered the visit that I had had in the bathroom. Surprisingly, drawing had taken my mind completely off of everything, and I had barely even thought of where we were.

The idea of wandering around the place, the possibility of stumbling upon something that I wasn't meant to find. The idea to stay hidden away inside my room, door closed and invisible to the rest of the world seemed much more simplistic.

"Why do you keep doing that?" She asked, a suspecting tone hidden beneath her words.

Huh?... oh.

I realized that I had been staring at her again, my eyes probably not even blinking.

My expression changed to something solid, as I took a deep breath.

"I'm sorry, Liz. It's just…" I paused. "Were you in the bathroom earlier? Like when I was in the shower?"

Her face changed to resemble something close to that of disgust.

"Why the hell would I be creeping on you in the shower?" She sounded angry, confused. "I wasn't even downstairs."

I decided to let it go. What was the point?

Most of me knew that there was no way that it would have been her, but a doubt in me wanted to believe it. I just wanted it to make sense.

There was nothing left to do besides admit to myself that I was either going completely nuts, or that there was some form of evil lurking in the house.

I wasn't sure which of those would be worse.

"Just forget it," I stated. "I just thought I saw someone."

She seemed to become intrigued, as the anger in her face turned to concern.

"What do you mean? Like who?"

"Nothing," I repeated, "It was probably no one."

But I knew that wasn't true.

She took a step toward me, seeming to be much more interested than I'd expected.

"What did it look like?" She whispered, her eyes beginning to tear up, as she glanced through the doorway behind her.

What? It? She must have seen something, too.

An intensity rose within the room as we stared at each other, shock smacking me in the face like a hard brick wall. Goosebumps formed over every inch of my skin, an endlessly-seeming shiver ran down my back.

I swallowed.

Do I even want to know?

"I couldn't tell," I choked out, my voice quivering. "It was just a dark shadow. It looked like a tall person... I saw it through the shower door. Maybe they had a hood on? Like a long sweater or something? The weirdest part was that whoever it was turned and disappeared, but the door didn't open at all and when I got out it was still locked."

She didn't move as I rambled on.

At first, I couldn't tell at all if she had believed me. She was always poking fun at me, never really taking me seriously, at least, that's how she was before the accident.

Her eyes formed a long and hard blink as she rose up a hand, rubbing the side of her face. It was almost as if my words had sparked some sort of realization in her.

Did she see something similar?

"I know it sounds crazy," I then added, hoping for her to tell me what thoughts were filling her head.

She let out a shivering sigh, her eyes still watering.

"Claire," she stopped again, hesitating as she spoke again. "... Claire. This morning I was awake so early because I swore I could see... I saw a shadow. It was standing at the foot of my bed, just staring at me. I went outside to get out of the house, hoping it would help but it didn't, really. I didn't tell you 'cause I didn't know if I believed it myself... there's something really wrong here. With this house."

My eyes grew wide in fear as I found myself turning to look behind me, expecting to see something sinister lurking just inches away. The only thing I could see was my drawing. The drawing of home, and I so, so badly just wanted to go back.

"I believe you," I whispered, turning back to face her. "Does this mean you don't want to walk around?"

I asked her in hopes that she would decline, that she would refuse and change her mind. At the same time, I wanted to find out what the *hell* was going on. Who, or what, was doing this? And why? Maybe the very answers we needed, and craved, were hiding within the walls of the house.

I suddenly remembered the photo that my mom had shown me, the one with the door, the glowing, eye-like reflection. Where had that picture been taken? I hadn't seen any rooms that resembled it since being here.

I suddenly grew an urge to locate it. I thought that maybe there was a chance that it was relevant to what was happening to Liz and I. I needed to find out why such an odd picture had been mixed in with so many relevant others.

More than anything, I just wanted things to make sense.

"No, I still want to. I mean, if you're still up for it," she answered, a nervous chuckle escaping her mouth.

"Yeah, sure."

I stood up from my chair and took a step forward, trying to figure out exactly where we were going to start, and then I remembered.

"My closet," I started, turning towards the locked door. "I don't have a key."

She moved a foot towards it, only slightly glancing.

"Oh, yeah!" She exclaimed, reaching a hand into her sweater pocket.

I could hear the sound of clinking metal as she fumbled through it, her hand moving around as if the pocket was a never-ending hole.

I watched as she pulled out a single, silver key and held it up towards me. There was smug look in her eyes that I didn't quite like.

"Here," she placed the key onto my open palm, pressing so hard I swore the metal was going to cut right through. "Mom said to give this to you. I thought it was the house key, but maybe it's for that?"

I walked to the closet door and stared at the door handle.

I wondered what we would find inside. Was it completely empty, awaiting my clothes and hangers? Was it full of old belongings, left behind to turn to dust?

As I continued to think, more gruesome and disturbing thoughts crept into my head. Was there a body, left half decomposed, hidden just behind? Was there another dead animal, as there had been in Elizabeth's room? Or maybe there was something much more ominous, waiting and preying on us to open the door.

I pictured a dark shadow, standing there as I would open the door, leaping out to attack the second the light would enter. Maybe it would grab me and Liz and simply drag us away.

I fluttered my eyes and shook my head, as if the visions would shoot out with the motion.

I pressed the key into the slot and turned, the lock unlatched with ease.

As I turned the handle and began to pull, Liz and I glanced at each other, and then back to the door in unison.

Slowly, the door creaked open.

There seemed to be nothing out of the ordinary. The closet was empty, and probably less that three feet deep. Cobwebs surrounded the ceiling inside, dust, coating the hardwood floor.

"Wow, spooky!" Sarcasm replaced the fearfulness in Elizabeth's voice.

I let out a sigh of relief, turning away and closing the door.

Studying Liz, I could see that she wasn't really frightened anymore, her expression was more intrigued.

I walked past her and headed for the doorway when suddenly, something made me stop dead in my tracks.

18

"Claire, where do you wanna-"

"Shh," I stepped slowly out into the hallway, holding my arm back, motioning for Liz to stay and wait.

"What is it?" She whispered, the sound barely escaping her mouth.

I ignored her, trying my hardest not to make a sound as I tip-toed across the hallway.

It didn't add up.

The sound of water beading against tile echoed throughout the hall. I could hear water being carried throughout the pipes, the slight humming of a tap.

As I approached the bathroom door, I noticed that my sister had ignored the hint, and was trailing right behind me.

"Claire, what are you-," she paused as realization hit. "Oh."

Setting my hand down on the door handle, I could feel the warmth against my palm.

The shower was on.

Shakily, I opened the door and stepped inside.

Steam filled the room like a heavy blanket of fog, musty heat fell upon my skin, causing me to sweat instantly.

I glanced over to see that the glass door to the shower was left wide open, inside, vacant.

We were the only ones in the room.

I made my way to the shower and reached in to turn the tap off, noticing that it had been cranked to the highest temperature possible.

The water subsided as silence fell.

I closed the shower door, a *click* echoing from the walls and back into my ears.

As I turned around, I noticed Liz standing, still, in the doorway. Her eyes fixed on the steam-covered mirror.

My heart began to race as I clapped a hand across my mouth, refusing to let out a scream.

I couldn't take my eyes away from the words written across that mirror.

What does this mean? What does any of this mean?

In that moment, I realized how surreal it all was.

I'M STILL HERE.

"Claire," my focus was broken by a low whisper from Liz, as my eyes darted to her, and then back to the writing.

"Claire," she repeated. "What does it want?"

A tear left my eye and I couldn't tell if it was caused from fear... confusion, or maybe even rage.

I stood up straight and marched over to the window, picking up the drying cloth from the rack beside it. Drying the mirror off, I watched as the letters disappeared.

19

"Let's go," I stated, heading back out into the hall.

I didn't know where I was going, I only knew that I didn't want to be in that room any longer.

Not stopping to wait for Liz, I stomped down the hall to the single other door that I hadn't opened since being there.

"Let's go. You want to see the house, right?" My voice was booming, anger rising within me.

I couldn't tell exactly what had set me off. Maybe it was the fear that I was trying so desperately to shove down, deep inside. Maybe the anger was caused by the mockery that this thing was trying to make of me. Maybe, just maybe I was so fed up with living like this, living in a house that even possible paranormal beings had wanted to rid me from.

"Come on, where are you?" I called out, my voice echoing loudly back at me. "I'm right here, you idiot. *I'm still here.*"

I found myself mocking it back.

Who cares how angry it gets?

"Claire..." my sister's voice arose from behind me. "Claire, calm down. You're freaking me out."

I turned to see Liz, eyes wide open, staring at me as if *I* were the monster.

Her face was pale white, her skin clammy.

Seeing how petrified she was, I realized that I had only made matters worse.

She needed me to be strong, not lose the little bit of sanity that remained.

She's only a kid. I told myself, forcing my rage to subside, only a little.

"Sorry, Liz."

I looked back to the door in front of me. "I'm still going. Are you coming?"

For a few short seconds, no reply came. And then she spoke.

"Yeah... Yeah, I'll come."

I pulled the door open as she crept up behind me, I could feel her hand grasp the fabric of the back of my sweater.

Her hand was trembling, her breath sounded unsteady.

"You really don't have to."

I tried to convince her not to bother, I didn't want to drag her around after what had just happened.

"No," her voice quivered. "No, I want to."
Fine then.

In front of me was a small set of carpeted stairs, the first piece of floor in the house that hadn't been hardwood.

I descended quickly, but slowly enough to allow Liz to keep up.

The room was dark, pitch black, even.

In the corners of the room in front of me, I could see two black shadows, standing straight and tall.

What the..?

I slid my hand against the wall, feeling around the wooden boards for a light switch.

My hand rubbed against something, as the room became showered in light.

There.

In the corners, I could see two suits of armour, standing straight up with large shields, and bearing swords.

They seemed to be almost life-like, as my eyes fixed on the hollow emptiness of theirs. Empty and black.

"I don't like those," Elizabeth's voice startled me, as she relaxed her grip on my sweater and then let go. "They're weird."

She stepped around me, heading towards the human-like suits.

She stopped right in front of one, peering into an empty eye-socket, her head leaning in so far I thought she would knock it and cause it tip it over.

I pictured it raising up it's arms, reaching out to grab my sister as it would entrap her into an overbearing maul.

"You just said you didn't like it," I exclaimed, my voice shaky. "What is wrong with you?"

As she ignored me, I watched her stick a finger right into the empty hole of the suit.

Her finger didn't even budge as she turned to me, a wide grin spreading across her face.

"It's fine, dummy," she pulled her hand away and formed a fist as she began knocking on the hollow tin. "Fake as all hell."

It was as if her attitude had performed a complete one hundred and eighty degree turn. What was she playing at?

"Alright, Liz. I'm done with this room."

As we toured the rest of the house, nothing seemed to be out of sorts.

There was a large, dusty, unfinished basement, where the laundry room was found. It was dark and dingy, but not unlike any other basement. Balls of old cobwebs swept across every inch of the ground.

There was a one-vehicle garage located right off the living room, attached to the house. It was mostly empty and smelt something like that of dirt, mould even. The only thing that sat about were a few boxes labelled 'dad's tools.'

A door leading to the attic sat just above the landing leading to my mom and Elizabeth's room. There was nothing extraordinary about what was up there. Sure, there were some old things piled up in the corners of the space, things that I thought would be fun to go through. An old chandelier, some boxes with no labels.

We decided that it was too much to do in that moment. I was tired, and I knew that Liz was exhausted from all of the unloading she had done previously.

I stepped down from the ladder, pulling the door closed behind me, it's heaviness making itself known throughout the stairs and hall with a large *thud*.

As I stood alongside Liz, I noticed something. The room from the photos could be found nowhere in the house. None of the rooms that we had looked at could have resembled it in the slightest. I glanced around the landing as if searching for another door, another hall. There was nothing else I could see, but surely it was somewhere.

My search was cut short as Elizabeth's voice startled me.

"So," she started, causing me to turn back and study her. "What are you going to do for the rest of the day?"

My mouth opened as if I were about to say something, but then quickly closed.

I had no idea what I planned to do.

At least, back in the city, there were places to go and people to visit nearby. There were sights to see, like the boats along the water, carnivals and pop-up events. There were things to do, like walk around the mall with friends, staring into the store windows, dreaming of outfits we would never buy.

Here, there was nothing. Endless trees that stood in the cold rain, uninviting to say the least. A creepy house that gave off the feeling of being trapped, alone. And a feeling much, much more threatening.

"Claire?"

I adjusted my eyes, as I discovered that I was entering a sort of daydream.

"I'm not sure," I answered, returning my focus to her. "There's not really much to do now. I think we've done it all."

She let out a slight chuckle, and then turned to peer into our mother's room.

I could hear my mom humming, as the sound of fabric falling onto the mattress filled the empty space.

She must have been unpacking, or folding laundry. I wasn't exactly sure.

"Okay, well, I'm going to go read a book in my room or something," she turned towards her bedroom, heading for the doorway. "I'll see you in a bit."

I fought back the urge to join her, to go sit inside her room with her, in an attempt to avoid whatever was tormenting me, but it seemed as though she wanted to be alone.

"See you in a bit."

I turned back, and headed down the stairs. As I entered the hallway, I found myself walking alongside one wall, keeping as far away from the bathroom as I could.

Heading for the kitchen, I walked passed my bedroom. Only slightly turning my head, the only thing that I could see inside was my bed, messy, as the blankets fell to the side and half onto the floor.

My stomach gurgled, loudly, as I resisted the urge to go and tidy up the room.

I shook the thought from my mind, focusing only on making my way to the kitchen to grab a bite to eat.

My eyes met the window as I turned into the room.

It was hard to see outside as I noticed that a thick blanket of fog lay across the ground, creating a cloud of mist. Through it, I could only tell that the sun had already set, only small amounts of light poured into the fog and through the layers of trees.

Removing my gaze from the window, I glanced over to the cupboards to see that one of them sat wide open.

I bit my lip as I stepped forward, placing my fingers around the polished wood door.

As I was just about to push it closed, I hesitated.

There was a faint sound echoing in through the hall. *Pish, click. Pish, click.*

I froze, trying to figure out exactly what I was hearing.

Pish, click. Pish, click.

The sound didn't seem to subside, as it only grew closer and more distinguishable.

Footsteps.

I found myself staring at the doorway, my eyes wide fingers beginning to tremble.

If only I hadn't seen what I had seen, then maybe I wouldn't have been so easily frightened.

"Liz?" I called out, my voice seeming so intrusive to the quietness of the room.

I half-expected no answer to come.

"Just me, Claire."

I felt a wave of relief as my eyes returned to the cupboard door, the shaking in my hands settled.

It was only my mom.

The sound of soft slippers against hardwood made it's way into the kitchen, my mother's silhouette appearing into the corner of my eye.

Closing the cupboard door, I turned to her to find that she was wearing pyjamas as if she were ready for bed.

"Sorry, hon. Didn't mean to startle you," her eyes met mine. "Are you hungry? Let me fix you something."

She stepped passed me and made her way to the refrigerator, pulling open the stainless doors.

The sound of bottles and bags filled the room as she moved things around, in search of something.

"Umm," I started.

"How about a sandwich?"

She didn't wait for me to respond as she began to pull out lunch meat, tossing it over onto the dining table.

I watched as she tossed items onto the table, and then proceeded to butter bread.

"Thank you," I stated, glancing back at the cupboard door, almost as if I had expected it to be open again. It wasn't.

"Not a problem," she answered. "Did you girls have fun today? Did you find anything interesting?"

She set the butter-knife down, glancing over to study me.

I stepped over to the table, trying to think of what part of my day I should tell her about. I made my way around the table and took a seat directly across from where she stood.

"Well..." I started, pausing for a brief moment. "Aside from the ghost in the bathroom, nothing really interesting."

I ran my fingers through my hair, setting it back into place, a few brown strands entangling themselves around my fingers. I shook my hand, letting them fall to the hardwood floor.

"A ghost?" My mother's voice cut through the stagnant air, a hint of mockery escaping within her words.

I looked up to her to find that she had an eyebrow raised, her eyes questioning me.

The sound of porcelain scraping filled the room as she slid a plate across the table, it landing right in front of me.

"I guess," I sighed, glancing down to the food she had prepared for me.

I picked up the sandwich and took a bite.

"I'm confused, Claire. Are you seeing things?"

My eyes met hers again as I fought to swallow down a dry lump of bread crust. I shook my head.

"No, I don't know. It's just weird here."

She studied me, squinting as if trying to make out the fine complexities of my face.

"Maybe we should bring you to the hospital again. Who knows what they may have missed..."

What? Does she think I'm going nuts? That this is all due to a bloody head injury?

The truth is that I felt completely fine. Sure, my arm was sore. The stitches on my face itched, but my head felt completely fine, without so much as a present headache.

"No, Mom. I'm fine."

She pulled up a chair and took a seat across from me, reaching down to her plate and taking a bite of her food. She looked as though there was more that she wanted to say, but instead she remained silent.

She set her dinner back down onto her plate and glanced up at me, and then to the clock behind her.

I yawned as I looked up to see that it was nearly ten o'clock. I could barely tell where the day had gone.

"Well," my mother started, forcing a long stretch, her arms in the air. "I'm going to go relax, I have a lot to do tomorrow. You should get some rest too, maybe you'll feel better in the morning."

I shrugged, watching as she stood up from her seat and set a plate down in the empty sink.

"Goodnight, Claire."

As she disappeared into the hall, I noticed what sent a wretched wave of disbelief straight through me.

I shivered.

The cupboard. It was wide open again.

20

I stood up from my chair, not bothering to push it back into place and darted to the doorway and down the hall.

Flicking on the light switch for my bedroom, I slammed the door shut. Somehow, the familiarity of my personal things made me feel a bit less anxious, and more at ease.

I pressed my back up against the door, closing my eyes and letting out a sigh of relief, as if whatever was happening couldn't just follow me. As if whatever this was, wouldn't dare enter into my personal space. A feeling of security, that probably shouldn't have been present at all.

Taking a step over to my bed, I turned and let myself fall down onto the mattress, the springs within, almost causing me to stand right back up.

That's it. I thought. *Maybe I should just stay in here from now on.*

I turned and picked up my cell phone, the light from the screen lacking brightness in the dimly lit room.

Still no signal.

It wasn't exactly as if I had expected it to suddenly retain bars, but rather that I'd hoped.

Laying back, I set the phone down on the bed beside me.

The light remained on as I closed my eyes and attempted to fall asleep. I tried to forget the happenings of the day, as they began to play on repeat throughout my mind.

I'm still here.

I tried so hard not to think about those words, but I so badly wanted to understand. What had it meant?

21

As I opened my eyes, I peaked over to the doorway. The hallway was dark, only the light from my bedroom illuminated it's walls.

I didn't remember falling asleep, but I knew that must have been the case.

But why did it feel as though I didn't sleep at all?

An unsettling feeling fell over me, as I glanced over to the window to find that it was still dark outside. My eyes settled back to the hall.

At first, I couldn't tell what seemed so out of place. Was it the fact that I had woken up so suddenly in the night? No.

I closed that door. I closed it, yet there it is. Sitting wide open.

As I picked up my phone from beside me, I discovered that it was nearly four o'clock in the morning. That explained why I felt like I hadn't slept.

Letting out a yawn, I rubbed my eyes.

I grasped the covers that laid over me and tossed them off to the side.

I was tired, but I knew that there was no way I'd be able to fall back asleep.

As I set both feet onto the hardwood floor, a sound echoing into the room made me freeze.

There was a loud thud, as if someone had dropped something, echoing in from the hall.

It sounded as though the noise had originated from upstairs and carried down to the main floor.

Maybe my mom was awake? Maybe it was Liz?

I so badly wanted to believe that was the case, but somehow, I doubted it.

Thud.

The sound came again and this time, I could tell that it was coming from upstairs.

I stood up from the bed slowly, my eyes not daring to break contact with the wall of the hallway. As I stepped out of my bedroom, the sound came again, but this time was different.

Thud-creeak. Thud-creeak.

Footsteps.

I inched toward the doorway, my eyes wide with fear, as I turned the corner and entered the empty hallway.

I glanced up the staircase, the sound of footsteps paused, and then carried on again.

Thud-creeak. Thud-creeak.

The sound was coming from above... it was coming from the attic.

"Liz..?" I whispered out into the hollow home, hoping she would respond. But as I suspected, no answer came.

The thought of going to her room, waking her and dragging her up to the attic to investigate with me, seemed so comforting.

I tip-toed up the stairs and to her room with the intention of jolting her awake, but stopped as soon as I saw her laying there, sound asleep. One of her legs hung off the side of the mattress, an armed curved up under her head. I didn't dare wake my little sister and bring her back into this nightmare of a reality so soon.

As I turned away from her bedroom, I focused my eyes to the small door just before stairs, footsteps still carrying on.

Ugh.

My arms trembled as I bit my lower lip.

Here we go.

Creeping over I reached out one hand, my arm still trembling as if someone were shaking it, vigorously. Before I could let any more ill thoughts enter my mind, I whipped the door open, a low-pitched *creeak* filled the empty walls.

It was in that instant that the sounds of an intruder completely stopped. Silence. I could hear nothing aside from the sound of Liz's snores, carrying down from a few metres away.

Click.

Without a single thought, my eyes darted into the foreboding darkness that blanketed the air just in front of me. I reached my arm inside the small room, feeling around for the string that had hung from the single light bulb.

The dim bulb flickered on.

I looked around, expecting to find the culprit of the sounds that were driving me crazy, my breath unsteady.

Where would a click sound have come from? And what were the sounds that sounded so much like someone walking around? Rats? A raccoon? Doubtful.

As the search of the room began, the sounds of boxes thudding filled the small space. Nothing of interest occupied any of them, some old cassettes, dusty blankets filled with cobwebs, old baby rattles and porcelain knickknacks.

"Who would leave all this junk," I muttered aloud, not expecting an answer.

"*You,*" a scratchy voice echoed out.

My head shot back in surprise, darting back and forth as I attempted to spot the intruder.

It was too small, there wasn't any possible way that there was anyone with me.

"What!?" I called out, slightly louder than I had intended. I wanted to say more, but my voice refused. Suddenly, I felt a surge of frustration run through my nerves, and without thinking I began to toss boxes and loose items, not caring anymore what could break.

The sound of cardboard on wood filled the room, as I slid the boxes up against the walls.

Am I going crazy?

Not sure what I was looking for, I kept searching. There had to be something in there that could lend even a slight explanation.

Wait a minute, what was that?

I could see a crease in the wall just behind a cardboard box that had been slightly tossed. Leaning over carefully, I studied the strange shape in the wall.

No way. It can't be... it almost looks like...

I shifted the box over again, and pushed it slightly to allow myself a better view.

Another door?

It was small, so small even a young child may have a hard time getting through.

I scooted myself over towards it, placing my finger tips against where there should have been some sort of doorknob. Nothing. No latch, no lock... It was just a flat square panel that would have been impossible to notice, if I hadn't been looking so closely. Pressing both hands against it, I suddenly felt a pressure let go, as the door clicked inwards and then popped open.

I swallowed.

Fighting a war within my own head, I tried to decide if i should go in, or just wait until morning to tell my Mom and Elizabeth. Knowing that I may have to face whatever entity had been causing so much chaos, I lowered my body, crouching down until I was basically laying down.

Peeking inside all I could find was more darkness, besides the one thing in the back of the room.

Glowing, red eyes.

22

Without allowing myself any sudden doubts, I forced my body in through the small doorway, my stomach scraping across the ground, my bad arm threatening to give out.

I let out a grunt, pushing and pulling my way in. The sensation of needles piercing into my forearm were present, as I winced and attempted to reach for my arm, to try to somehow comfort the pain. Toppling onto my side like a limp worm, I decided it was no use.

I have to make it through this door. I'm not going to let this stupid arm get in my way any longer...I swear when I get out of here, I'm going to march straight into the kitchen, grab the sharpest knife I can find and cut this damned thing off.

It seemed as though hours had passed before I entered the dusty room. Resuming my gaze to the two lights that sat just ahead, I found myself staring, their soulless glare returning to me.

As I pulled myself up, slowly, from the ground I did not dare look away.

I wiped the dusty residue I could so clearly feel all over my palms onto my pyjamas, the linen between my fingers being the only calming thing in the moment.

"What do you want?" I managed to choke out, my eyes beginning to adjust to the darkness, ever so slightly. "Who are you?"

No reply.

The lump in the back of my throat began to grow as I attempted to swallow it down, as if it would somehow just disappear as well as all of my fears.

Still, I could make out very little in the room. The area around the strange thing I was looking at was noticeably darker than the rest of the room, like a shadow surrounding what seemed to be eyes.

A hooded figure? Something demonic, staring at me, daring me to join? There's no plausible answer.

"H-Hello?" I whispered again, scanning the floorboards with my hands. The feeling of twenty years worth of settled dust coated my palms and fingers, I patted the dust off on my lap, doing nothing but transferring the dirt onto my night gown.

The eyes hadn't moved, as I decided to begin forcing myself towards it. Dust covered my bare skin and clothing, as the old wooden floorboards threatened to break apart and jab themselves into my skin.

Ow.

A small sliver of wood broke free and lodged itself into my thigh, sending a shivering pain throughout my leg. My gaze broke from the two lights just feet away, as I uselessly attempted to swipe the pain away. There was no use, it was much too dark to see anything. The whistling of the wind against the old house siding was unsettling and loud in the eerie silence.

I looked back up, expecting to see bright red lights glaring back at me, but to my surprise there was nothing there.

Huh?

Here I had been hoping I would approach the lights to find it was just an old television, but there was now nothing there at all. The glowing lights had vanished in the split second and a half that I had managed to break my stare.

I quickly moved myself down to where they had been only seconds before, throwing my arms out in front of me and feeling for anything, but there was nothing there. Emptiness was all that stood.

I quickly spun myself around, my eyes scanning the room, trying to see anything that sight would allow.

There was nothing.

Screeeak.Click.

The sound of a light door closing filled the empty space, as I began to hear the boxes of miscellaneous items being shimmied around in the attic. I scooted my body down attempting to get out.

My fingertips feeling around the small door I had used to get into the hidden space, I could feel it had been tightly closed. There was nowhere to get my fingers around to pry it open... *it was being held shut by something.*

As my hands scanned around the only chance at an exit, I began to hear something behind me. The sounds of fabric rubbing along wood and bones scraping could be heard, but I did not dare to turn around.

With my heart racing, and a flash of heat sweeping over me, I quickly moved my hands up and down along the door. It was no use.

It won't budge.

Without hesitation, the terrifying sounds behind me grew closer. I spun my feet around my body, and began to kick the wood panel.

"Help!" I screamed, my bare feet hitting the wood so hard I expected it to crack. "Liz, help me!"

Perspiration poured down my cheeks. I could feel a presence growing closer. The little hairs on the back of my neck stood up.

Shit.

I felt the fingers of death grip onto my shoulder, hard just like a boulder and as cold as winter snow. I let out a blood curdling scream, that I couldn't even believe had come from my own mouth.

"NO! Let me go! Liz...mom...help me!" I couldn't stop screaming. It refused to let go, fingernails as sharp as needles, penetrating my flesh.

Suddenly, a slight stream of light began to enter the small, dark space as the door pushed against my palms, forcing it's way open.

"Claire?"

I could hear Elizabeth's voice echo in as the hand removed it's grasp and retreated back into the darkness behind me.

"Fuck. Liz run, move. Let me out!"

I felt myself growing hysterical as I tried to understand what exactly had just happened. Pushing my way out of the space, I noticed a look of concern come over my sister's face. I didn't dare stay in there any longer. I nudged my sister out of the attic and pushed my way out.

Back outside Liz's room, everything seemed quiet again. There were no sounds of footsteps, nor talking, or even the sounds of anyone's snores filling the house.

"Claire, you're.. you're bleeding!"

I barely noticed Liz's worried words as I began to walk into my mother's bedroom.

"We can't stay here, Liz. We gotta go! We have to leave now," I exclaimed. "We have to get out. Mom? Mom, we need to leave this house. There's something very wrong here."

Approaching her bed, I could hear Liz trailing quickly behind me.

"Where is she?" Liz asked, her voice quiet and mouse-like.

I stared at the bed. The covers had been balled up on the mattress, the pillows on the floor.

Something isn't right.

I glanced over to the balcony window to find it was clearly way to early for my mother to have gotten up already. And if she had, why would she have deliberately ignored the commotion in the attic and my pleading calls for help.

"Mom!?" I called out. My sister wrapped her fingers around the back of my shirt, as she began to call out too.

"Mom, where are you?"

Moving as quickly as my trembling feet would allow, I began checking every corner of every room, peering off the balcony and even strange spots like under the beds.

My mother was nowhere to be found.

Back in the kitchen, I poured myself a glass of water, pouring out another for Liz. There was no hiding the concern in her expression, as I could see her eyes wide in horror.

My stomach felt as if it were tied into a knot, goosebumps settled over my limbs.

"Claire," Liz's voice broke the stale silence. "What...what happened in the attic?"

I felt a shiver, as I tried to decide how to explain what had just happened. I didn't even believe it, myself.

"Just... don't worry about it Liz. We need to find Mom, and leave."

Setting a glass of water down in front of her, I took one to the other side of the table.

Liz's eyes went from wondering, to dread and defeat, as she peered down at her drink.

"Where the hell is Mom?" She asked, her fingertips rolling the glass as she refused to break her gaze.

23

As I set the empty dishes into the sink, I let out a sigh.

I reached over and grabbed a pair of boots and a light jacket, and peered out the window, observing the light rain. A light layer of fog covered the ground as the sun attempted to peak out from above. There were few birds out, and it was still mostly dark. Slipping on my jacket, I peered up at the clock to see that it was nearing five o'clock in the morning.

"You're not going anywhere without me," Liz stated sternly. "Like hell am I staying in this house alone."

I let out a sigh, realizing that she was right, and there was no way I was letting her out of my sight. Not right now.

"Get your coat on then, I'm going to see if I can find any sign of where Mom went."

"Be right back, don't go without me."

She ran out of the room suddenly, and returned with a set of purple boots and a denim jacket.

Peering back out the window and over towards the garden, I noticed something, her gardening gloves. They were set down on the lawn chair, a trowel covered in fresh mud sat aside them. It looked as if she had already been outside gardening.

Weird.

"Come on, Liz," I mumbled, heading straight for the side door.

As I stepped outside, I could hear my sister trailing closely behind me.

I glanced around the yard, searching for anything that could explain the absence, or where she could be.

I watched as a squirrel climbed up the dying bark of an old pine tree, it's little feet scratching away at the wood as it climbed. I glanced in the direction of the well, then to the back of the property, then towards the trees of the front yard that we had driven through.

"Can we go towards the road?" Liz whispered, biting her bottom lip. "I'd feel better checking that way first, and then at least if we do see a car, we could flag them down to call someone for us. Even to call Dad or just... I don't know."

Something about her pleas and strange way of thinking actually made sense. If Mom was actually missing, then having someone else on the outside, aware, could be nice. Maybe they could use a phone, or at the very least, get a ride into the closest town to use a phone there. There was also just something comforting about seeing another human being in the midst of all the chaos and supernatural things that seemed to be happening.

"Yeah, you're right. Let's go that way."

We started our journey towards the road, even though I knew it would probably take us at least thirty minutes to walk all the way out there.

Leaves crunched beneath the heels of my boots, as Liz's footsteps followed with the same sounds closely behind.

Crunch....crunch...crunch...crunchhhh.

"Wait, Liz, stop for a second," I whispered, setting my arm out towards her chest, gesturing for her to stop in her tracks.

Crunch...crunch...crunchhhh.

Fuck. Why.

Shifting my gaze from tree to tree, I tried to find the source of the sound.

Crunch.

This time it was closer.

I turned my head back towards a pine tree, when suddenly I could see a shadow in the near distance. A cloaked figure stood just behind a bent spruce, and even though the hood seemed to cover it's face completely, it wouldn't take a rocket scientist to see that it was watching us.

"Liz," I choked out a whisper, as I could see her peering over into the same direction. "Liz, we need to run..."

The figure stepped out, taking a step towards us, but still a generous few meters away.

"Liz... RUN. To the road, go!" This time my words were much louder.

We turned in unison and darted towards the front of the property, fear rushing through my blood, as my heart pounded so hard it felt as though it would burst within my chest.

"Claire... what is happening?" She asked, her voice breathless, words choked out through exhaustion.

"It doesn't matter, what matters is we need to run."

What felt like forever seemed to pass, as I found myself glancing around, checking beside me, and then turning my head to check behind us.

There was no one there anymore. It stopped chasing us... but where did it go?

As I turned my glance back towards Liz, I felt a sharp pain shoot through my ankle, a cracking sound filled the air, as I stumbled down to the leafy ground.

"*Aaahhhhhh,*" The sound of Liz's shrilling scream could be heard.

"What *happened?*" I muttered, my eyes closed, as I tried so hard not to focus on the pain in my leg. I could hear Liz just behind me, sobbing as if she was in pain too.

I sat up and stroked my ankle, attempting to lessen the pain, but seeing it now, it was turning purple and definitely was beginning to swell.

Just what I needed right now.

"Claire..."

I turned myself towards Liz, forcing myself to ignore my ankle.

"Claire it's the, he's the.. it's..."

Her words were so choked that they were hard to make out.

"It's what, Liz?" I asked, trying to see what the big lump was that lay in the grass in front of her. "What is that?"

As she looked up at me, her face grew white as snow, her lips a purplish hue. I watched her, as she turned away and vomited in the direction away from me.

"Liz, what the fuck. Are you alright?"

I leaned onto my hands I forced myself to stand up. As I placed pressure on my ankle, I could tell that, thankfully, it was not broken. I forced myself over to her. When I glanced down and saw what it was that was laying in front of her, my stomach tied itself into a knot.

I suddenly felt very weak.

I turned away from where Liz stood. And I couldn't help but vomit, too.

24

The flesh was so stale and decomposing, that it was very clear, the body had been there for days. As I studied what was once skin, I could see the meat peeling away from the bones, gashes from where the crows had feasted riddled spots that used to be plump, live flesh. Maggots filled body cavities that hadn't previously existed, worms wriggled their way through and around what was once eyes. A mouth wide open, in an almost horrified expression, exposed a decaying tongue and blood stained teeth. What was once such an inviting, lively face, was now a lifeless, soulless shell of a body.

Trying to find signs of a cause of death, I scanned up and down the empty body, but could find nothing. It seemed as though he died so horrifically, and yet we heard no screams. No sign that it happened at all. Surely, we should have heard his cries from the house.

This poor bastard. If only he had known his fate. Surely, he would have never even allowed himself to enter this property at all. Why does this feel like it's my fault?

I allowed my mind to race, trying to think of all the things that could have been done differently to help this young man avoid his fate. I just couldn't make sense of what had happened.

Looking up, I could see that Liz was just as perplexed and horrified as I was. My poor baby sister. She looked at me in horror, as I watched a tear trickle down her cheek.

"We are going to die here, aren't we Claire?"

Shocked and in disbelief of everything that was going on, I glanced around to make sure we were alone. There was no sign of the shadow figure anywhere.

Although neither of us wanted to be here alone, *at least we were alone again.*

"We are not going to die."

I'm sure the pause in my answer didn't make her feel reassured. "Let's keep moving."

As we started our way back to the road, I held her hand in mine, squeezing gently in an attempt to assure her I would keep her safe. Our eyes locked for a moment, and I could tell that she was petrified.

The twinkle of something shiny within the tree line caught my attention, as I quickly glanced over to see what it was.

A car. It was the cab.

"Liz, do you see it?" I exclaimed, removing my hand from hers, and jogging over towards the vehicle.

She said nothing as she followed, musty leaves crumpling beneath our feet as we hurried.

The driver's side door was wide open, a sweater hanging out of the car, and random contents spread across the ground. Kneeling down, I picked up a cell phone and examined it.

It had been smashed, the screen cracked to bits to the point that there were chunks of the glass missing. I pressed the side button, attempting to turn it on, but it was completely destroyed.

"Ugh, of course," I mumbled, there was a *thud* as I dropped it back down to the dirt.

"What's wrong?" Elizabeth asked, peering over my shoulder. "Oh."

She sounded as defeated as I felt.

As I inspected the car, I noticed that the tires were all slashed, each one sitting on the rim. The back window was smashed. Shards of glass were scattered across the back seats where we had sat just days before.

I looked over to my sister to see her tearing up, and biting her lower lip. I quickly glanced back to the vehicle. My eyes locked onto the driver's seat.

Without thinking preemptively, I sat down in the seat, looking around for... I don't even know what. Surely there was something that could help us...

I began by throwing open the glove box, followed by the centre console... nothing but paperwork and a pack of cigarettes.

"Fuck!" I gave up, slamming my head down against the steering wheel, and shutting my eyes. I let out a huge breath of air, as I could hear the wind brushing through the branches of the trees, leaves swaying down to the ground.

I took a deep breath and held it for a moment, and then let it out. As I felt the air escape my body, almost seeming to push away the fear I felt inside, I slowly opened my eyes.

I began to attempt to brainstorm a way out of the mess. I could hear the crunching of the leaves beside me, as Elizabeth adjusted her footing. But, other than that, everything else stood silent, almost ironically casting a slight feeling of peace.

What can we do now? Where is Mom? Oh, I just need Mom. Where is she?

Finding my mind filling with unanswerable questions, I forced myself to snap back into reality. A reality I wished was a bad dream.

I focused my eyes on the gauges that sat behind the steering wheel, the feeling of leather pressing into my forehead, pressing into my cuts.

I let my head back, removing it from the steering wheel and looked outside of the car to Liz. Her eyes didn't meet mine, as she stared down to her feet.

She's probably nearly defeated.

As I was about to get out of the car, I peered over to my right to notice a speaker connected to some wires. My eyes felt like they nearly fell out of their sockets.

It was hard to picture that young lad having a CB radio in their car, much less that he would have actually used it.

"Elizabeth, look!" My voice cut the surrounding silence, sharply.

I could feel her lean into the car beside me, her shadow casting over me, her breath shaky against my shoulder.

Reaching over, I picked up the mic and held it under my chin, as my other hand began twisting the knob in attempt to find an open channel.

Static. It's all static. I continued to scan, passing so many channels that I must have checked them all at least twice.

"No, no... no!" I barely meant to cry out. "What is happening? Stop, stop, stop! This can't be real!"

My voice was hoarse, the words just pouring out from within me.

This is it. I am going to go mad. I will be truly insane.

I listened and, watched in anguish, as my fingers continued to twist the little black knob, nothing but the sounds of static and faints sobs could be heard.

I could feel the hope I held onto begin to whither away.

Liz set her hand gently on mine, pulling my hand off of the radio, and taking the mic from me. She gently set it back down in it's place.

"It's going to be okay, Claire," her voice was settling. "I promise."

I wanted to believe her so bad, but so much doubt festered within my mind. Dread filled my bones, as I could feel hopelessness overtaking me.

I held Elizabeth's hand in mine as she helped me back out of the car.

Forcing myself to hold my head up, I could see in her eyes that she was horrified. It was easy to see that she was on the brink of tears.

"Let's go, sis. We're gonna figure this out. Let's go find help."

It was weird to see Liz trying to take charge of the situation, as that role had always been mine.

"Yeah, we're gonna be okay. I know we will," and I didn't even believe my own words.

Hand in hand, Liz and I marched through the trees again, heading towards the road and away from the house.

"*Waaake up,*" the faint sound of a voice behind us in the trees could be heard, it was so faint that the exact words were hard to make out. "*Come back, Claire...*"

My body shook as, a chill shot down my spine.

I looked over to Liz. I could see that she was becoming more frightened.

Crunch. Crunch. Crunch.

I caught a glimpse of the road just ahead, as the sounds of intrusive footsteps began to echo out from the near distance behind us.

I turned to see a shadowed figure standing behind one of the dying evergreen trees. It didn't move, as it seemed to watch and even taunt us, in a way. Its face was taken over by shadow, and I wondered if it even really had a face.

Glancing over, I could see that Liz had spotted it too, her gaze aiming in the exact direction of the figure. And then I glanced back.

Gone.

"Where did it go?" I looked back over to Liz, to see that her jaw was hanging, her mouth open wide in disbelief. "Liz?"

She closed her mouth and then turned to look at me. It was hard to determine the thoughts that filled her mind in that moment.

For a moment, we paused and just stood there, looking at each other.

"It looked like it just..." Liz's words trailed off, as she started to walk towards the road again. I followed. "It seemed like..."

She couldn't find the right words to say.

"It just what, Liz?" I bit my lip.

"It seemed like it vanished into thin air... but I know that can't be right. Oh, God, Claire. I'm so confused. I feel like I'm going crazy."

We both knew that couldn't be possible.

"Well," I started, as we approached the gravel that lined the side of the road. "If you're crazy... then so am I."

In that moment I felt that I'd rather be crazy, than face the fact that all of this was really happening.

Somehow, standing on the gravel, away from the house and confinement, made me feel more free. I peered down the empty highway as some hope restored itself within me.

"I'm sure someone will come by and help us," I thought out loud.

Liz only glanced over at me, then back to the road as she bit her fingernails. Her body was visibly tense, as she anxiously waited for anything to happen.

I found myself repeatedly looking over my shoulder, almost expecting to see someone watching us again... but thankfully, the trees stood still, and empty.

And so did the road.

25

At least an hour had gone by as Liz and I sat together alongside the road, her body laid against my side, as I held her tight in my arms.

Not a single car drove by, which seemed very odd, and there were no neighbours for miles.

"This isn't working," Liz grumbled, as she pulled my arm off of her and stood to her feet. "We need to do something else."

I knew she was right, although I could only wish this torture would just end there.

"What do you suppose we do?" I asked. I could feel tiny rocks digging into my flesh, as I pushed myself up from the gravel and stood beside her.

There were no more plans I could come up with, my mind was like a black canvas; too stressful and full to add any colour.

"I'll go. I can walk to the closest neighbours house, or town. I'll get help. I'll call the police, or bring someone back here. Or, I'll wait here and you go. But someone has to stay in case mom comes back."

Her plan wasn't a good one by any means. But it was the *only* one. It *had* to work. There had to be someone that would be willing to help.

Letting out a sigh, I placed a hand on Liz's shoulder and smiled gently at her.

I turned back, and glanced the way we had walked and decided, that it was best for her to get out of here. I couldn't let my baby sister stay on these seemingly haunted grounds, all by herself.

"Okay. Mom said there was a town just up that way," I said, pointing a finger to the right. "Just keep walking straight. Don't stop for any cars by yourself. God knows what could happen. Just go straight to town please?"

Liz Smirked.

"Don't worry, Claire. I'll be careful. I'm going to walk to town, directly to the police station, and demand they help us."

I was proud of how brave Liz had become. It was hard to believe that when we started this move, Liz and I didn't get along at all and now we were inseparable. Having her back was the only highlight of this awful nightmare.

I reached over and took Liz into the biggest hug I possibly could, squeezing her tightly, just as if I'd never see her again. For a few moments, i refused to let her go, and I hugged her just as if I could transfer all of my strength into her body.

Worry filled my mind of different frightening scenarios that could happen, although very unlikely.

I pictured some creep, driving up on her just to throw her in their car and drive away, never to return. I thought of someone driving by, not expecting her to be on the road and hitting her with their car. I pictured her just walking for all of eternity, never to find a town at all.

As random thoughts filled my mind, I realized that I needed to stop thinking of these things. There was no point in getting all upset and worked up over very unlikely situations that my mind had made up.

I released Elizabeth from my entrapping hug, as I noticed a tear falling down her cheek and wiped it away.

"I love you, Liz," I smiled, although I'm sure she could see, that hiding behind it, was nothing but fear. "It's gonna be alright. You're gonna be alright. I promise. Just hurry back as soon as you find the police."

Liz nodded.

"I love you, too, Claire."

There was a long pause of silence before Liz turned around and began to walk away, leaving me behind, stranded, and all alone. I watched until I could no longer see her, as she disappeared into the foggy distance.

Oh... shit.

Realization dawned on me as I turned to face the wooded area.

I'm alone. I'm completely alone in hell... or am I?

And I wasn't even sure which was more terrifying.

At first, I didn't dare to move as I just stared at the empty area filled with nothing but trees. There were no birds flying about, there were no squirrels jumping from branch to branch. It was as if there was no sign of life anywhere. Except for what was left of me.

Without allowing myself to have second thoughts about it, I stepped a foot towards the house, and another, and another.

Crunch... crunch... snap.

I picked up my pace, running now as fast as my legs would allow, not daring to turn around or try to see what was approaching.

Refusing to allow myself to stop, I kept running, and running... and running.

* * *

Back in my bed, I hid beneath the covers.

I could hear the sounds of light, shuffling footsteps, pacing back and forth within the hall. I didn't bother to try to find out what it was. I knew it couldn't be anything good. And I longed for it to stop.

I just want to wake from this nightmare.

Hours must have passed as I laid there, not daring to move the blankets off of my head.

I couldn't shake the vision of the cab driver's lifeless body from my mind. I kept picturing his pale, blue skin. I saw insects devouring rotting flesh.

As I was being tormented by graphic photos appearing within my mind, I barely noticed that the shuffling sounds had stopped.

Is it gone? I wondered...

26

I forced my mind to become silent, as I slowly slid the blanket off of my face. At first, I could only lay there and stare at the ceiling, hoping that the sounds wouldn't come back.

"Claire."

I could hear a distant sound, as though it were coming from outside. A woman's voice? It was hard to tell.

I peered towards the door, slowly throwing away the rest of the covers and climbing out of bed. I tip-toed to the door, not daring to make a noise. I could tell by the sound of my own breath, that my heart must have been beating out of my chest, as I reached for the handle.

Slowly, I forced the door open, and peered out into the darkness.

My eyes took a moment to adjust, as I made my way around the house.

Everything stood silent. There were no more eerie sounds, no voices, no footsteps.

"Is someone there?" I whispered out. "Mom?... Liz?"

I made my way into the kitchen, and I was finally able to see a lot better. And I wished I hadn't. In that moment, I wished that I was blind.

Oh my God.

A dark figure stood at the door that led to the porch, it's silhouette overtaking the entire window. I couldn't make out any features. It was like something from a horror movie, but much more frightening.

As I stared at the entity, chills ran down my spine repeatedly. Until, I felt a sudden burst of courage. Enough courage to speak.

"Who are you?!" I shouted, my words echoing off the walls. "What do you want?"

My fear turned to rage. I could feel my blood pressure escalating, as I stared at the being, awaiting a response.

And then, suddenly, a wave of terror fell over me. I thought of trying to fight, but my body only wanted to run.

As I turned back towards the doorway, in an attempt to flee, to find a place to hide – what I saw, I could never forget.

It lifted up an arm, a bony, white finger protruding from within it's cloak. And it pointed it right at me.

Me. It wanted me.

As I turned away and ran from that room, I could see it following me. It was trailing me, walking almost as fast as I could run.

"Stop it! Go away!" I managed to shout.

I ran down the stairs and into the living room.

As I stumbled into the room, and looked around for anywhere to hide, I could still feel the presence approaching. It was inching closer, and closer with every passing moment.

As I could hear it nearing the top of the stairs, I scrambled to wedge myself in between the bookshelf and the wall. It was such a tight space that I nearly fit, but thankfully, I did. Just barely.

I held my breath, as I squeezed my eyes shut, and waited for it to come and get me. My heart was pounding, and I prayed that it wouldn't hear it.

"Claire." Its voice was hoarse, raw even. *"Come out little girl. You can't hide from us."*

My eyes shot open, and all I could see was the polished wood panels of the wall, my forehead pressed against it's cold exterior. I clapped my hand over my mouth, in an attempt to mask the sound of my sobs.

Just go away. I thought, closing my eyes again. *Just leave me alone, already.*

My thoughts were pointless.

27

Every hair on my body stood on end. I could feel it standing right behind me. I could feel it's eyes embedding themselves into my very soul. I could feel it's malevolence growing, only inches away from me. And I could feel it, growing closer, and closer. My body trembled in terror.

I didn't dare to open my eyes, as I felt it's bony, sharp fingertips press into my shoulder. I could feel my flesh separate beneath its razor sharp talons, as I let out a pleading cry. My hand shot up in reflex, and as I reached up to my shoulder, I could feel it. It's hands were cold, and felt of rubber... and they were damp with blood. My blood.

"You can't go anywhere, Claire. You'll never get away."

It's voice did not sound human at all.

I covered my ears, and began to shout.

"Just tell me what you want! Just tell me! I'm *fucking* done being afraid!"

As I shouted, a burst of courage fell over me. It only lasted for a second before it turned to dread again.

Suddenly, I realized that I could no longer feel it's hands gripping me anymore. No longer could I feel it's chipped and torn fingernails pressing into my skin. And I realized, that the entity had left.

Or so I thought.

28

Slowly, I let my arms down and opened my eyes. I could feel no presence standing near, as I daringly turned my head to face the room.

I let out a sigh of relief, as I realized that the only silhouettes to be seen were that of the Victorian suits of armour.

For now, it seemed as though I was alone, again. But I knew that the entity was still there. That it was just waiting to come back and finish what it had started.

The more I thought about it, the more I didn't understand. Surely, it didn't want to kill me, because if it did, I was sure I would be dead already. There was nothing stopping it from just slicing away at me, emptying out my veins until there was nothing left. Easily, it could have just strangled me and cut off all of my air supply, leaving me to choke on my own throat.

Why didn't it? I asked myself, wincing in confusion, and then in pain.

My shoulders throbbed, as I felt the blood trickle down my arms. I looked down to see that my cast was now covered in blood, along with my shirt.

I pulled the fabric of my shirt away from my shoulders, to reveal deep, dark lacerations. Blood poured from them, as I placed my arms across my body, attempting to stop any further blood loss.

I started to feel dizzy. The room became fuzzy, as my body threatened to lose consciousness.

I headed for the stairs, barely able to keep my balance, as I wobbled from side to side. My arms caught the banister, as my legs tried to give way beneath my body. But, still I pressed on.

I hobbled up the stairs and hurried towards the bathroom, my arms scanning around to use the walls and furniture as my guides.

I threw open the cupboard, and began searching for the first aid kit. My arms scanned inside the empty shelf, coating it's interior with my blood.

I could barely see anymore, as things began to go darker, and even darker. My hand knocked over bottles that I assumed were soaps. Worthless bottles of soap.

Where the fuck is it? I thought, a mixed feeling of rage and fear overtaking me.

Finally, I found a washcloth. It wasn't what I was hoping for, but it was going to have to do for now.

I backed away from the cupboard, my legs so unsteady, that I collapsed to the floor. I sat up against the wall, and pressed the dry cloth to the shoulder that I felt must have been bleeding the worst.

What now? Where is Mom? God, I hope Liz is okay... I don't know if I can do this anymore.

I knew what I had to do. The only way out now, was going to be to leave. I had to head into town after Liz, and find her. Find Mom.

I thought about what could have happened. It didn't make sense that Liz wasn't back yet, and I could only hope that she was okay. I could only pray that nothing had happened to her. I wondered why I didn't just go with her. We should have both just gone together.

I stared at the tile floor to bathroom. The static-like feeling of being faint wouldn't subside, and I felt so tired. I felt cold. I fought it for as long as I could, until I realized that I couldn't fight it any longer. And I let myself drift away. Into nothingness.

29

Slam. Bang.

Huh? I forced myself to open my eyes, despite the weakness I felt. The faint sunlight that poured through the window above my head reflected off the floor, however dull. I could hear the distant sounds of the morning birds singing.

For that split second, I forgot. I forgot about the torment that had happened during the night, I forgot that my family was missing, I forgot that my shoulders had been practically torn away. How on earth could I have forgotten about that? Even if just for a moment.

Creeeak.

I could feel the vibration of heavy footsteps entering the house.

Bang.

The door slammed shut.

I barely had enough energy to get up, and as I looked at my hands, I could tell they were much whiter than normal. I wondered how much blood I actually had lost, and I knew that the answer to that could not be good.

With my entire body fighting me every step of the way, I pushed myself up off the ground, using the porcelain towel rack to help support myself.

"Liz?" I called out.

The sounds were not the same as the apparition that had followed me, no. These were much louder and more physically apparent. But, no one answered my calls.

"Mom, is that you?" I tried again.

Still no answer.

As I stood, my body resting, mostly up against the tile wall, I forced myself to take a step. And then another.

The bleeding from my shoulders had slowed, but the pain was still immense. I winced, as I forced myself on.

The footsteps grew closer as I neared the doorway, and made a run for it. I set my feet down on the hardwood as gently as I could, so as not to be heard. But the footsteps continued on. Louder and louder. Closer and closer.

I decided in that moment, that the only place to go was out. I wasn't sure where I would run, but I just knew that I *had to get out of the house.*

I made my way around the dimly-lit house, stumbling as things threatened to go dark again.

No. I can't pass out now. I'm almost there.

As I reached for the handle of the kitchen door, I turned my head to see that it had caught up, and was most definitely trailing right behind me.

But this was not the same thing that I had encountered... this was something else. Something that seemed much, much stronger.

As I locked eyes with this monster, it had locked eyes with me too. Those red, glowing eyes that materialized from beneath it's dark, torn cloak. It's body cast a large shadow, it's feet, hidden beneath what looked like fabric. As it's eyes threatened my soul, I could see a smile, filled with razor-sharp teeth, begin to spread across it's pale, white face. It's skin was peeling, it's teeth stained red with blood.

As I expected the smile to dissipate, it only grew larger, it only became more masochistic. And I could tell, that it enjoyed every second of tormenting me.

Why won't they just stop?
I asked myself, as if I had expected an answer to appear.

For a moment, I questioned why I was fighting so hard. I thought of maybe just letting it take me. But then, I was filled with a sudden surge of energy, adrenaline pumping it's way through my blood, forcing my will to live.

"Fuck you," I taunted, as I stared into it's blood red eyes.

And I watched it's smile recede immediately.

I turned for the door again and threw it open, as the entity ran after me. It moved with unworldly speed, as I stepped out onto the porch.

As I ran across the porch, I could feel the wood crackling beneath my feet, but I barely payed attention.

My foot caught a loose board as I attempted to get away, and sent me falling to the ground.

"ahh," I let out a yelp, as my stomach made contact with the ground, knocking the wind out of me. My jaw hit the ground, causing my teeth to hit together. A wave of pain shot throughout my body.

As I lifted my face up, I pressed myself up from the ground and quickly got back up.

This isn't how I go.

Glancing behind me, I could see that the entity was still behind me, but it was moving very slowly. Clearly, it was toying with me.

I reached for the banister and rushed myself off the porch, and ran towards the trees. I wished I had ran towards the road, but thinking quickly, I ran the opposite way, deeper into the forest.

Maybe if I can get deep enough into the trees to lose it, then I'll be able to find my way back around. Maybe there's still a chance to get help and get out of here.

I knew that my thoughts were mostly in vain, but I had to try to convince myself. I knew that if I didn't, I would lose all the hope I had left.

As I scurried, I could see it following still, but much further behind.

The sunlight attempted to light my way as it rose from a distance, it's beautiful rays of calmness pouring in from in between the rows of trees. Birds flapped their wings above my head, diving in and out of the branches. The rustic colours of falling leaves filled the ground, as my feet crunched them to bits. The sounds of squirrels and birds echoed throughout the forested area, bringing me a small sense of calming and comfort.

But it was still behind me, and I knew that it meant me harm.

30

Branches and leaves crunched beneath my bare feet, splintering into my skin. Cold mud caked the bottom of my feet and in between my toes.

I fought against the pain in my shoulders, and the pain in my jaw as I continued to run.

I made my way deeper, and deeper into the trees. Suddenly, I noticed that I felt very much alone.

My foot caught a large branch as I nearly tripped, but managed to regain my balance.

I stopped.

As I placed my hands on my knees, and bent down to try and catch my breath, I could feel that the monster was gone. At least for now.

I walked over towards a large, solid tree and collapsed beside it's trunk. There was something soothing about this tree, as I realized how far from the house I had actually ran. I felt alone, but at the same time, something about this tree reminded me that everything was going to be okay. If this tree could sit, solo, for so many years and still be so strong, then why could I not?

I rested my head against the tree and peered back towards the way I had come from. There was no being in sight. And for a split second, I felt peace.

Just breathe, I told myself. *Everything is going to be okay.*

The area where I rested was dark, overcasting branches blocked out the majority of the sunlight. Small bugs flew about, as I attempted to swat them away from biting at my cuts. Tiny sharp pains soared throughout my limbs, as they continued on biting.

Just a tiny rest. That's all you need... Just five minutes...

Despite the agony that my body was in, and the fear that filled my head... I allowed myself to fall asleep.

* * *

"Claire," Liz said, as she poked my nose with a pencil, a huge smile sat upon her face. The feeling of her soft mattress beneath me was so comforting, as I looked at her. I smiled back.

"So for this assignment, we need to look up some shops in New York City," I answered her, as I looked at the papers that were placed upon her lap.

This was familiar. I remembered helping her with that essay she had to write for school on the five boroughs of New York, and which shops were the most popular.

I looked at the papers, and then back up at Elizabeth. She looked back at me, her eyes wide and her expression blank. It was as if she was staring directly through me.

"Claire," she shouted, jabbing the pencil into my nose repeatedly. "Claire... Claire... Claire.."

* * *

My eyes darted open to see a robin sitting upon my chest. It was poking at my nose with its beak, practically biting at me.

Trying to ignore my grogginess and let my eyes adjust to the light, I had almost forgotten where I was. In the middle of nowhere.

"Claire," I could hear someone calling in the distance.

No, not again.

I refused to sit there and wait for another – or the same – entity to come and find me again. I was done letting them play games with me. I was done being their toy.

The robin chirped, and then flew away, heading back up toward the treetops.

Thanks, little guy, I thought, watching him fly away. *Be free.*

As much as the biting had hurt, I was sure that if that little robin hadn't woken me, I would have been screwed.

I stood myself up, and attempted to wipe the dirt from my pants. That was no use.

"Claire!" The voice was getting closer, maybe only a couple of yards away now. "Claire!"

I ignored it as much as I could, and headed away from it, as I disappeared deeper and deeper into the forest.

As I got further away from the house, the trees seemed to become bigger, fuller. There were tons of fallen branches and unkempt grass and weeds littering the area. And as I hurried further, the walking path became unclear.

I had to take another way, and hope it would somehow lead me to safety.

"Claire," the voice was much closer now.

I had to move faster.

I entered a clearing in the trees, the area was filled with huge, moss-covered rocks instead. Stumbling over them, I noticed a silhouette emerging into sight behind me.

Shit.

I didn't look this time. I didn't want to see which one was now following me, and I didn't want to find out if there was another.

I picked up my pace, forcing my legs to climb over top of the boulders.

Finally, once above the rocks, I discovered that there was another clearing. It was flat dirt.

"Claire, stop it!" I heard it call out. But I didn't dare to slow down, or turn around.

"No! Leave me alone!" I shouted back, as I forced my legs to run at full force across the dirt clearing. I wasn't going to let it get me.

And that was my mistake. I fucked up.

By the time that I had realized that my feet had hit the top of that small cliff, it was too late. It was probably about fourteen or so feet down, but it caught me so off guard that the way I fell, there was no way to change the outcome.

My feet hit the small rocks that sat atop the escarpment, and I reached my arms out, as if trying to grab hold of something invisible to change the fate that I was about to experience.

"Claire, no!" The voice was right behind me this time.

I could feel a strong arm graze my elbow as it twisted me around to face it. And, as I fell, I realized I had made the biggest mistake I could have made.

Dad. It was my Dad.

He bore a look of anguish, as I fell. We locked eyes, and I knew, that even without words, this was us saying goodbye. This was the first time that I had seen him in months, and the last time that I would ever see him.

I'm sorry, Dad. I love you.

I had no other thoughts in those last moments. I didn't feel scared, I didn't feel anything, besides guilt. I couldn't believe I had been so wrong. I should have recognized his voice.

As I hit the bottom of the dirt, I felt my bones shatter. My head hit with a loud thump, and sheering pain filled every part of me.

As the life left my body, I could see nothing but my father. He watched in sorrow as I slowly slipped away, and there was nothing he could do. He was powerless.

And right before everything went dark, I could see a being appear from right behind him. It was the entity that had chased me into the trees. And it was right behind him.

I watched in horror, as it reached it's hands out from beneath it's cloak, and took my father in it's arms. I watched as it stole him from me. The last bit of hope I had left at all.

It's maniacal smile burned into my eyes, and settled into my brain.

And that was the last thing that I saw.
Before I slipped away.

31

Beep. Beep. Beep.

"Oh, my God, she's waking up! Nurse!"

My entire body felt paralyzed, as I attempted to gain the strength to open my eyes, but I couldn't. The only thing I could move was an index finger, at first.

Footsteps approached, and I could feel something suddenly grabbing at my arm, lifting my sleeves up and pressing against my wrist.

Get off me, I wanted to scream. *Don't touch me.*

But no words came out, I couldn't even open my mouth.

"Claire. Claire, honey. Are you awake?" A woman's voice appeared, echoing inside my head like that of a hollow house. "Claire? Can you open your eyes?"

Just let me sleep.

I ignored them at first, refusing to even try. I attempted to rest my thoughts again, and fall back asleep.

Suddenly, I could feel a pressure on my eyes, as they were forced open, the muscles in my eyelids fighting them every step of the way.

That was when I felt the scorching of light being shone through, directly into my pupils. My retinas felt as though they were on fire.

I wanted to scream.

"She's awake," the voice spoke, again. "Can I get some damp towels?"

"Sure," another voice answered.

Just leave me alone, I internally begged. *Stop touching me.*

It was almost like they had heard me, because for a moment, they stopped.

But only for a moment.

Warmth encompassed around my neck, and then on my forehead, making it difficult to try to rest anymore.

My eyes flickered open, almost automatically.

The brightness of the room burned my eyes, as if I were staring directly into the sun. I closed them again, and then squinted them back open.

Struggling to see felt was like having a war with myself at the time.

At first, I couldn't tell who was in the room with me. I could only make out shadows, and very few colours.

Soon enough, my sight began to clear as I could see who was standing at the foot of the bed I laid in. My father.

This can't be real, I told myself. *I saw that thing get him. I practically watched him die.*

I stared in confusion, as everything else in the room became more clear.

There were two nurses standing on either side of me. They were checking monitors and wires that were hooked into my veins, pulling some out, and adding new ones in.

I forced myself to forget about everything else that was happening, as I stared into his eyes.

His facial expression showed concern, and something that even looked like fear. He didn't break eye contact, even when I did.

"D-dad...," I choked out, my throat dry and my voice hoarse. "Are you okay?"

The nurse that stood to my right let out a chuckle, as I turned to look at her.

"You're the one in the hospital bed, my dear," her words sent confusion throughout my mind, yet her voice, itself was soothing.

I knew that I was in a hospital bed, but what I didn't understand was how on earth I had survived that fall. I felt my bones *snap*. I felt my skull *crush*.

32

"Okay, Darling. You can sit up," the nurse with the brown hair assured. "Let me help you."

She took hold of my arm and helped me stabilize myself so I could sit up.

I couldn't say much. I was in shock.

I looked at my father, my eyes burrowing themselves into his.

What the hell happened?

A tear rolled down my cheek, as I watched the raindrops trickle down the hospital window. It was odd how the weather always seemed to match my mood.

I tried to connect to my Dad through my thoughts, hoping he would somehow be able to tell, just by my eyes, what was going through my head. Just in case, maybe there was something he couldn't say in front of the others.

But it didn't work. He only stared back at me in concern.

"C-can I get up?" I asked, pushing myself up out of the bed, regardless.

"Oh, hon, not so fast! Quick, grab me the wheel chair."

One nurse spoke, as the other followed her instructions and placed a wheelchair directly beside me.

"Okay, Claire. Let me help you over."

She placed her arm beneath my underarms and helped me to the chair, the second nurse balancing my other side.

"There you are," she stated.

Sitting in the chair, I felt trapped. It was like a cell without bars, a cage without a lock.

I wondered for a moment if I had injured my spine or something of the sort, causing me to me paralyzed. As these thoughts began to throw me into a sort of panic, I wiggled my legs and torso and found that there was no noticeable numbness. I was fine.

I reached my hand up to the back of my head, to find that there were no cuts. Looking at my arms, I could see a lot of bruising, and cuts that laid in a consecutive pattern. They didn't look consistent with a fall. They seemed more like something you would expect to come from claws, or talons.

Claws. Sharp fingernails.

Flashbacks of the hooded figures flowed through my memories, as I shut my eyes tight, and then reopened them.

I was safe now. There was nothing to be scared of. I was out of that God forsaken house, and with my Dad. I wasn't alone anymore.

I looked up at my father again, partly expecting his expression to have changed, but it didn't. He remained silent, as he only stared at me with emotional pain in his eyes.

"What's wrong, sweet heart?" He asked, his eyes watering.

I wasn't sure how to respond.

There's so much wrong.

"D-dad," I managed to choke out. "What happened? W-where's mom? Where's Liz?"

I missed them so much. I needed to talk to them and find out what had happened. I needed to make sure they were okay.

Are they here too?

He didn't speak, as he looked away. I could tell this time that he was hurt, as the sounds of his muffled sobs filled the room. He buried his face into his hands.

"Claire, when are you going to stop?" His voice was almost completely drowned out by tears, as he tried to fight them back.

"What- what do you mean?" I asked, concern now growing within me, too.

"I'll be right back, just hit the button if you need anything," one of the nurses stated, as she stepped outside of the room, the other nurse followed.

My dad didn't answer, he only nodded.

My confusion quickly turned into rage, as I threw myself up from the chair. As I stood up, I felt a sharp pain shoot up my leg, and I looked down to see that there was bandages covering both of my legs.

Maybe the fall wasn't as bad as I thought.

I forced my legs to hold my weight, as I fought on.

My father could barely even look at me, as I stumbled passed him and into the bathroom, using counters and objects to help steady myself.

I turned the tap on and cupped my hands with cold water. As I splashed the cool water on to my face, it felt almost as if my soul was returning to my body. It was like waking up from a really deep sleep.

I looked up to the mirror to inspect my face, and see how bad my scars were.

Shockingly, the cuts that I had previously were barely visible. They were old, and white as if they had healed years ago. It didn't make any sense.

What the fuck?

I leaned in closer to the mirror.

Something wasn't right. This wasn't me. The face staring back at me, was that of a woman. Slight creases were visible at the ends of her eyes. Her forehead had several wrinkles, and her hair was slightly greying.

I let out a small scream.

"Claire, are you alright?" My Dad asked, coming around the corner and peering at me from the doorway.

"Do you see that?!" I yelled, pointing towards the reflection. "Who is that? Who the *hell* is that. What's going on? Dad?"

I began to ramble, and started to feel as though I'd go completely insane.

He placed his head in his palm. No answer.

"Talk to me! Tell me what is going on? Where's Mom and Liz...?"

My father sighed, looking up at me as I returned my gaze to him.

"Claire, I can't do this anymore," he whispered. "You *know* what happened. This hurts me, too, ya know."

I didn't understand.

"Just *tell* me."

He stepped into the bathroom and stood beside me, gesturing for me to look back into the mirror, as he did, too.

I noticed that his reflection, too, was not how I had remembered. His hair was almost completely grey, he had so many fine lines that made up his face that just weren't familiar. His eyes even seemed as though they had lost colour, like they were empty.

"Look," he started. "That's me, and that's you. Claire. This is the last time I'll have this conversation with you. Your mother and your sister died in that accident seventeen years ago. You were lucky to make it out alive. You had severe head trauma, and you developed hallucinations. We've been through this so many times before. I love you, but I can't do this anymore."

As I stared at the mirror, into our reflections, my head began to whirl. I placed a hand up to my cheek and I could feel that my skin was much softer, looser, than I remembered.

This... can't... be...

I tried to convince myself, but the more I thought about it, the more I began to remember...

The accident. They pulled me out... I saw my mother and sisters' lifeless, blue bodies laying in the grass. I had broken my arm and had lacerations to my face and body, and I must have broken my mind. I was in the hospital... I remembered that they fed me pills, they made me eat slop. They put a white jacket on me so I couldn't move. They made me feel terrible, and worthless. They treated me like a joke... they locked me up.

And then... I ran away. I remembered when they came at me with that needle to sedate me, they wanted to stick it into my vein. So, I ran. How could I have predicted that when I ran across that street that car would hit me? I couldn't have known it would come barrelling around the corner. And then there was a bang.. and then pain.. and then things went black. Yes, I'd been here for years.

"Oh. My God..." my voice was almost a whisper.

As I snapped back from my thoughts, and looked over towards my Dad, I realized that he was no longer there.

"Dad?" I whispered, glancing around the bathroom.

There was no answer, at first.

As I stared at the doorway that led back to the hospital room, I began to feel that dark, threatening presence. It was horrendously familiar. That sickening, terrifying presence.

I didn't dare look away.

"D-dad..." I whispered softly, "N-nurse."

I knew it was no use.

I conjured up the courage to walk towards the doorway, and I peaked my head out towards the empty room. There was no one in sight, and the place stood eerily silent.

"Da..."

As I tried to call out for him again, for him to come and help me, I felt that torturing feeling, that I so wished I'd never feel again.

It's cold, dead hands gripped tightly at my shoulders.

"Please, let me go," I cried.

But it's fingers only dug deeper as it whispered into my ear, it's hot breath burning my skin.

"I'm still here."

About The Author;

K.G. Miceli is a newly published author from the Windsor, Ontario, Canada area.

With five published books so far, she hopes to one day reach the minds of many.

She started out her writing journey as a child, but began to dive deeper into her work after the passing of her first son. She has built a community, *Angels Above Us,* a page located on Facebook, where many individuals go to read and speak about their losses with other fellow grievers.

She enjoys working on her own and with others, and would love to hear any feedback you have.

She has a wide range of genres; spanning anywhere from horror, to poetry and children's books.

"I'm still here," began in the summer of 2020. It took almost four years to write, and was one of K.G.'s stories that she had wanted to write for years before starting.

Follow on FB – Author K.G. Miceli

Follow on IG & Threads – k.g.miceli

Follow on Tiktok - @authorkgmiceli

Find me and follow on X, Amazon, Goodreads, Fable & more.

For rights and permissions, please contact:
K.G. Miceli
authorkgmiceli@outlook.com
F.B. - Author K.G. Miceli